I only said I couldn't cope

Dr. Celia Banting

Wighita Press
P.O. Box 30399
Little Rock, Arkansas, 72260-0399

www.wighitapress.com

This is a work of fiction. Names of characters, places, and incidents are products of the author's imagination and are used fictitiously and are not to be construed as real. Any resemblance to actual events, locales, organizations, or persons, living or dead, is purely coincidental.

Library of Congress Cataloging-in-Publication Data

Banting, Celia
I Only Said I Couldn't Cope/Dr. Celia Banting – 1st Edition
p. cm.
ISBN 0-9786648-2-5 (paperback)

1. Therapeutic novel   2. Suicide prevention   3. Grief   4. Depression

Library of Congress Control Number: 2006928586

Layout by Michelle VanGeest
Cover production by Luke Johnson
Pictured on cover: Part of the Burghers of Calais sculpture by
Auguste Rodin, 1840-1917

Printed by Dickinson Press, Grand Rapids, Michigan, USA

Issues addressed in this book:

Suicide prevention

Grief, despair and depression

Rituals: The role of a funeral

The child as care-giver

A pathological need to please others

Negative family dynamics

Guilt, self-blame and forgiveness

Defence mechanisms (projection)

Adhering to negative life "decisions"

Reckless behaviors related to feelings

How shock impacts upon cognitive functioning

Guided imagery to explain disassociation

Cognitive development and the perception of reality

Exploration of the concept of life after death

Exploration of the concept of life before life

Dr. Kubler-Ross: The "grieving process"
(Denial, Anger, Bargaining, Depression and Acceptance)

Consequences of negative rumination

The role of memories in the "grieving process"

Accepting the unfathomable

Finding peace

Dedicated to Erica Elsie, and my dear husband Des

Acknowledgments

My grateful thanks go to my proofreader and typesetter, Michelle VanGeest, who frees me from my dyslexic brain, and replaces my mother's voice. Thanks to Bev, my stray-word spotter, too. I thank my dear brother, Steve, for his computer expertise, and my wonderful husband, Des, for the inspiration and support he gives me. Thank you to Luke and Sam for their faith, inspiration and talent. Thank you to my dear friend Vicki for her guiding sense of style.

Thank you to all my psychotherapy tutors and colleagues at the Metanoia Institute, London, for teaching me about human nature, psychopathology, growth and recovery.

I thank the good Lord for giving me a lively imagination, and I also thank my parents for moving to the Isle of Wight, "the land that bobs in and out of view, depending upon the sea mist."

Chapter One

Today's Saturday and I've been waiting for this day to come for ages; it's Becky's birthday and she doesn't know it, but I've organized a surprise party for her.

Becky and I have been going together for nearly two years. Her mom and dad had a hissy fit when we first started going out, as we were only fourteen, but after a while her dad started to like me, and then they didn't seem to mind us going together. He suddenly started to like me when he realized that I went fishing, and every time I called for Becky he'd go on and on about rods and reels. I'd have to stifle a grin as Becky stood behind him making faces and using her hands to exaggerate the size of the latest fish he'd caught.

My mom didn't seem to care about Becky and I going together; all she ever said was, "Don't you go getting yourself into trouble, or her into trouble for that matter." Did she think I was a little kid or something? Anyway, two years down the line, everyone's used to Becky and me being together.

Her mom and dad are great. In fact, I prefer being at their house more than mine. Mom's always in a mood. Dad left when I was eight, and since then there seems to be a war going on in our house. I have two older sisters who hate each other and who fight all the time. Nancy, the oldest, says that Sherrie is jealous of her because she's got a good-looking husband and three cute little kids. Sherrie isn't married but has had loads of boyfriends, all of which Nancy says terrible things about. I think I can see why Sherrie might be jealous of Nancy, but sometimes I think that Nancy is more jealous of Sherrie. Girls—I don't get them.

I've got three little brothers. Jed is my real brother and he can be a real pain. The other two have different dads who visit the house sometimes, and when they do we all have to get out. They give us money and seem more interested in Mom than in the boys.

For as long as I can remember, Nancy and Sherrie have always argued, and when Nancy still lived at home I managed to keep out of their arguments, which seemed to happen every day and over nothing, as far as I could see. Who cares whose turn it was to wash the dishes or put the trash out. Jed and I didn't seem to fight in the same way they did, even though he was a pain sometimes. I'd just clip his ear and, being three years younger than me, he'd shape up and that would be the end of it. But not the girls—their arguing was constant.

Even though Nancy doesn't live with us anymore, she's always here. I don't mind though, because that means that Tom's around. Tom's my brother-in-law, and he's the coolest person I've ever met. When I'm a man I want to be just like him. He likes to live in the fast lane. He dresses cool, and women seem to flock around him. Sometimes Nancy gets mad, but he just blows her off, and after a while she calms down. She always ends up apologizing to him. It's smooth how he deals with her. I want to be like that.

The thing I like the best about Tom is that he has time for us boys. Ever since my dad left, there's been no one there for us to do guy-stuff with, and up until a few years ago before Nancy met Tom, the house seemed to be filled with girl-stuff—Mom's, Nancy's and Sherrie's. It's not easy being in a house where women seem to rule and we boys are pushed aside, but when Tom started to date Nancy everything seemed to change. I can't ever remember my real dad doing guy-stuff with me, like kicking a football, going fishing or going to a game, so when Tom came on the scene it was great because he started doing those things. He used to take Jed and me fishing, and although we never caught anything, he'd show us how to put a worm on a hook, while Nancy squealed, and we reveled in making her feel squeamish. We sat for hours on the riverbank trying to ignore them kissing, hoping to feel a tug on our fishing lines.

Sometimes Tom would take us out without Nancy, and those were the best times because he showed us stuff. He said that he'd been in the Marines. He showed us how to make a fire in the woods and how to trap rabbits. One time when Mom let us go camping with him, he showed us how to skin a rabbit and cook it over a campfire. Nancy was grossed out when we got home and told her. It made me laugh to see her nostrils flaring, and she started making gagging noises as I told her every detail about pulling out rabbits' guts. "Stop, Adam, quit, you're making me sick to my stomach," she'd cried, but Tom grinned at me from behind her, his face urging me to make the story more graphic. What is it with girls that they don't like boy-stuff?

Tom was always at our house and his presence seemed to make Sherrie even more bad tempered, and now that I'm sixteen I think I understand. I think she liked him even though she was always saying hateful things about him. I think she wanted him and was jealous of Nancy, for none of Sherrie's boyfriends were as good as Tom.

I remember when they got married. Sherrie was a bridesmaid. I don't think Nancy wanted her to be, but Mom said she had to ask her or else there would be a war in our house. The wedding photos showed everyone smiling except Sherrie, who was scowling.

I think that Mom was glad when Nancy moved out because Sherrie suddenly had no one to argue with, and even though she picked on us boys, suddenly the house seemed quieter. But frankly, life was harder for me after Nancy and Tom got married, because for a while they were busy and didn't come around so much. I knew what they were doing; I was only thirteen, but I wasn't stupid. Within a year Kelly was born, and suddenly they were around our house again all the time.

By that time Sherrie had finally found herself a boyfriend who would put up with her temper and moods, and having someone for herself seemed to improve her temper, so she was easier to live with and didn't seem to be so jealous of Nancy.

As Kelly screamed more, Jed and I got our Tom back, and he took us sailing, shooting and fishing. He filled our days with tales of his days in the Marines and showed us how to survive in the woods. If it's okay for a boy to love a man, then I loved him. He was my world; my hero and I worshipped him. When I was thirteen I wanted to be just like him, and now, as I stretch in my bed at age sixteen, and it's my girlfriend's birthday, I still want to be just like him.

I haven't passed my driving test yet, so yesterday Tom took me to the restaurant while Becky was out, and we met her mom and dad to work out the final arrangements. I felt excited with the secrecy of it all, and I could see that Tom was enjoying himself, too. We had it all worked out. Her mom was to take her out during the day, and Becky believed that her parents were going out in the evening and I was going to take her to the movies. Tom and I were going to pick up the cake and her birthday balloon, then he would drive me to pick her up, drive past the movie house and head for the restaurant. We'd tell her that we'd missed the start of that movie and would go for a soda to wait for the next one. Then as soon as we got through the restaurant door, everyone—hidden from view, all her friends at school and all her family— would leap out at her and sing "Happy Birthday" to her and give her presents. I know it sounds corny; but I don't care. I love my girlfriend, and I don't care if it isn't cool to show her how much I love her, I'm going to do it anyway. I want her birthday to be cool.

I scratch my head, yawn, and turn over, wanting to sleep some more, but the clock tells me that I've already overslept.

I can hear the little kids arguing downstairs. Since Nancy left to get married, there's no one to give them any attention and so they fight all the time.

My mind's so full of what Tom and I have planned for today that I can't be bothered to get up and sort them out. I hear Mom shouting, "Shut up, will you, you little..."

There she goes again. I don't know which was

worse, Nancy and Sherrie arguing or Mom shouting at the little kids. I think I'd preferred my sisters fighting; at least they were old enough to stand up for themselves.

My stomach turns over, remembering what it felt like to have Mom shouting at me when I was little. I get up and head towards the stairs, bleary eyed.

"Hey, what's going on?" I shout, hoping that Mom will take the hint and leave the little ones alone.

She shouts at me and I wish I'd left it alone, but something inside me can't. They're just little kids. I venture down the stairs, my mom's voice echoing around the house.

"What's going on?" I say again, rubbing sleep out of my eyes.

"Look what they've done," Mom complains. "They've trashed the place."

I look around. I can't see any difference; the place always looks trashed.

"Mom, go and take a shower," I say. "I'll take care of it."

I push her gently away; I know she's already lost it. I'm tired of it all, but standing before me are two little kids who didn't ask to be born. I kneel down and try to calm them down, but they're hyper and wild. Food, that'll get their attention.

"Who's for pancakes?" I say, raising my voice to get their attention.

"Me."

"And me."

"Come on, let's go," I tell them, walking into the kitchen. How come little kids will do anything for you if you occupy them? They love "cooking," yet all I get them to do is stir the mixture in a bowl and when the pancakes are cooked they squeeze syrup on them, but they love it, and never give me any trouble. How come my mom doesn't know that? It seems easy to me. Why does she have to get into an argument with them, when making them shape up is as easy as making pancakes?

My mind's only half on making pancakes as I'm thinking about everything I have to do to make Becky's birthday great, but the kids force me to attend to them. A thought flashes into my mind as I wonder whether Tom had to force himself to pay attention to Jed and me when we were younger though he had Nancy on his mind. I smile to myself as I realize that, when Tom was in love with Nancy, he'd have been thinking of everything other than the fishing or camping that my dad should have been doing with us, and I realize that I am the same as Tom. I'm trying to provide something for my little brothers that isn't there, just as Tom tried to provide something that wasn't there for Jed and me. The thought makes me smile as the boys argue over who's got more syrup, and it makes me more determined to follow in Tom's footsteps. I want to be just like him; he is my hero.

The kids are fed and Mom has put her makeup on

and obviously feels better. Now I can begin to think about myself and how to make this a special day for Becky. Everything's planned; I just have to make it happen. I hand the boys over to Mom, who looks bewildered and checks her hair in the mirror, as I head for the shower.

I'm excited as the water runs over me and slides down towards the drain. Today is going to be great. I love Becky so much. I've saved all my money to buy her a locket, one that says "I love you" inside it, and although I'm sure she'll like it, it's the surprise party that makes me most excited. I love surprising people; it makes me feel good inside.

As I towel myself dry, I hear a commotion downstairs and babies crying; Nancy and Tom must have arrived. When Kelly was one year old Nancy gave birth to twin girls, and since then she's always seemed a bit stressed out. Sometimes she snaps at Tom and accuses him of not helping enough.

Kelly runs over to me as I come down the stairs. I swing her high above my head and she giggles, drooling all over me.

"Hi, Adam, are you ready to go?" Tom says.

I put Kelly down and head for the door as Nancy calls, "Don't be too long, I need you here."

As we walk towards his car, he says, "Y'know, Adam, sometimes your sister can be a real nag. D'you want to drive?" He throws me the keys.

Tom's been teaching me to drive and I'm doing

pretty well. I pull away gingerly and feel more confident as I drive down the road and head towards town.

"I don't know what's going on with Nancy," Tom says, as I concentrate on checking my mirror and signaling to turn. "Ever since she had the kids, she seems to have changed. Sometimes she seems to be just like Sherrie, moody and bitchy, and constantly harping about something. Sometimes I just have to get out of the house."

I don't know what to say so I just keep driving.

"Even my dad's noticed a change in her. He said, 'She's turning out to be just like your mother.'"

Even though Tom's parents still live together, they seem to hate each other, and I've often wondered why they didn't get a divorce. But Tom said that they've always been that way and it's just how they are with each other.

He tells me to pull into a parking lot.

"We've got plenty of time; let's go bowling," he says.

"Okay," I say. Cool. I love bowling.

We decide to play five games and he beats me three to two. Eventually we leave and head towards the store to pick up Becky's cake and balloon. I've had a great day and I feel excited knowing that it's going to get even better during the evening.

As soon as we get home, Nancy launches into Tom. I'm embarrassed, and don't know where to look.

"Where have you been? You've been gone forever. I needed you here to help me with the kids. Mom's gone to work and I've got the boys to look after as well. Why didn't you take your phone? You did that on purpose so that I couldn't get hold of you, didn't you?"

I walk out of the room with Kelly trotting after me; the family room's a mess. There's food all over the floor and the boys are throwing cushions at each other.

"Hey, hold up," I say, as sternly as I can. "Quit that. Go out in the back yard and play. Go on." They look as if they're going to give me trouble but think better of it, and charge outside hooting and hollering. When I get married I'm only going to have two kids; I never want to live like this.

I tidy the room, trying to stay out of Nancy and Tom's way. She's giving him hell and he doesn't say much. Eventually she blows herself out and starts crying, and he walks into the family room with the twins, one on each arm. "See what I mean?" he whispers and rolls his eyes. He flips on the TV and begins to watch a game.

Everything seems to calm down after a while. Tom has a couple of beers while the game's on, and he cranes his neck trying to see the screen as the kids dart in front of the television, running in and out of the kitchen looking for snacks.

Nancy is making dinner and tells the boys not to

eat junk or they won't have room for their dinner. She sounds like Mom.

When the commercials come on, I phone Becky's dad. "Everything okay?" I ask.

"Yes, Becky's out with her mom and they should be home soon. Did you get the cake and balloon?"

I tell him that I did, and I can tell that he's as excited as I am. Becky's so lucky to have a dad like him; it must be great to have someone there for you all the time, not only to keep you safe but to make things exciting and special for you. I suffer a brief pang of envy but remind myself that I have Tom, and he makes up for not having a dad. He's my hero and I know he'd do anything for me.

When the game finishes I take a shower and get ready; I've got a new shirt to wear. We have to pick Becky up at six. My stomach's beginning to churn and I pray everything will turn out exactly as we've planned it. I can't wait to see her face.

I hear Mom come home, and she's ambushed by the boys wanting treats, and Kelly is crying to be picked up. The twins cry just to join in all the noise. Yeah, when I get married I'm only going to have two children; it gets too hectic with more. Mom gives them some candy, and they rush out into the yard, while Nancy tells Mom that they won't eat their dinner.

I look at my watch and it's five thirty; it's time to leave.

Just then I hear a piercing scream from the back yard. I rush down the stairs and follow Mom, Tom and Nancy outside. Kelly's fallen from the swing, landed on a broken bottle and there's blood everywhere. Nancy's crying, the twins are crawling towards the door crying, and Kelly's screaming. I feel sick.

Tom picks up Kelly, and there's blood pouring from a deep gash on her leg.

"Get a towel," he barks at Nancy. "Hurry."

Nancy seems stunned and I get there first. I rush back out into the yard, and Tom ties the towel around Kelly's leg, even though she's thrashing about.

"We have to get her to the hospital," he says, taking charge. "C'mon. Now!"

I don't know what to do, and I feel guilty for thinking about picking up Becky on time when my little niece is hurt. Nancy grabs her purse and tells Mom to take care of the twins, before rushing out of the door to follow Tom, who is already at the car. I follow them, feeling awful as I grab Becky's cake and balloon.

"Nancy, sit in the back and hold her leg tight," Tom tells her. "Adam, you sit in the front."

He makes me feel a bit better, and I love him for it, because I'm feeling awful with a birthday cake in my arms and a balloon bobbing above me as Kelly screams in pain. I yank the balloon and force it into the front of the car, which isn't easy as it keeps trying to get out of the window.

Tom drives like a madman. We screech down the road and along the highway, and I'm scared I'm going to drop Becky's cake as he swerves into the hospital parking lot.

They jump out of the car and run towards the emergency room. I put the cake on the front seat and trap the balloon, which seems to have a mind of its own, in the front of the car and slam the door shut. I follow behind as they rush into the reception area, where a nurse takes Kelly from Tom. They follow. I sit in the waiting area, worrying. I'm scared. I feel sick. I hate blood, and I hate the fact that my little niece is hurt. But what I hate most is the churning in my stomach at the thought of being late to pick Becky up for her birthday surprise.

My stomach churns so badly that I have to go to the bathroom, and all the time I can hear Kelly screaming. I hate how I'm feeling, and I'm sure that my anxiety is making my breath smell. I breathe into my cupped hands to check my breath and can't be sure if I'm just imagining things. I wanted every-thing to be perfect for Becky and now it's going to be ruined. I feel so ashamed and scold myself. What kind of person am I to be thinking of what *I* want when a little kid is scared and in pain? I feel really nauseous, and I'm glad I haven't eaten.

I go back to the waiting area with my head spin-ning. There are people everywhere, some with bandages on, others throwing up, some coughing, people limping, and even some people shouting at the nurses demanding to be seen by a doctor before other people. There are kids everywhere, all acting out and yelling. I want to slap them and tell them to behave, and as I have these feelings, I realize that I'm stressed.

I glance at my watch again. I'm late, and I hate being late. I can't sit still so I pace the floor, dodging the kids that are charging around. I'm so irritated that I want to kick them out of my way and unload my frustration onto them, but of course I can't, so I keep pacing. I drink from an ice-cold water fountain to relieve the dryness in my throat and for something to do. The noise seems to escalate. Suddenly I think I hate children; they're everywhere, and their parents aren't doing anything to stop them charging about. Perhaps they think that if their children irritate other people, they'll be seen quicker by the doctors just to get them out of the place.

"Excuse me!" I say uncharitably to a child who collides into me, yet he darts off oblivious, to my sarcasm, but his mother shoots me a dirty look. I don't care. My head feels as if it's in a fog, and I realize something's going on inside me that isn't the real me. I care what people think of me; I hate to hurt anyone. I'm never ugly to other people; I try really hard to be nice.

I read the notices on a board about garage sales and church fund-raising, trying to take my mind off the fact that the time is ticking by and the perfect evening I've planned with Becky's parents is going more wrong by the second, yet there's nothing I can do about it.

Eventually Tom comes out into the reception area, looking pale and shocked.

"They've got to take her to the operating room because the glass has cut a tendon, and if it's not fixed she could lose the use of her leg."

He looks awful, close to tears, and I don't know what to say. His hair is drenched in sweat and he attempts to brush it from his forehead.

"Look, man, I'm sorry you're going to be late to pick up Becky..."

"Hey, forget it," I say, trying to sound more reasonable than I feel. "It's okay. When you're ready. I'm just sitting here. When you're ready, okay?"

Indecision flashes across his face.

"Well, Nancy's here and they've just given Kelly a sedative to calm her down, so I guess we can pick Becky up, and I can take you both to the restaurant and still be back before Kelly goes into the operating room."

He seems to be talking to himself, and I'm ashamed to say that I don't say anything that will stop him from getting me to Becky's house, where I know she's waiting alone.

"Okay, that's what we'll do," he says, and he walks off to let Nancy know where he's going.

Moments later he emerges through the doors. Kelly's screaming has stopped, and with his car key in his hand he tells me, "Come on." I follow him out of the hospital, with shame, anxiety and excitement churning in my stomach.

I battle with the balloon again as I open the door, for it seems intent on escaping. I pick up the cake and set it on my lap while the balloon sticks to the roof of the car. Tom starts up the car and pushes his foot to the floor, and I feel the engine roar beneath me.

He sees me glancing at my watch.

His voice has a hollow sound to it. "Look, I'm sorry, okay? I know how much this evening means to you. I'll get you there as quickly as I can."

I don't know what to say. It's true, this evening means everything to me, but I'd feel selfish agreeing with him when he's so worried and would rather be at the hospital with Nancy and Kelly.

We race down the road, and he screeches to a halt, as the lights turn red. While he's waiting for them to turn green, he revs the engine with his foot and taps the steering wheel impatiently. As soon as the lights change, he charges down the road only to be stopped at the next red light. He cusses under his breath and I'm starting to feel really anxious. I grip the cake firmly but the balloon bobs about untamed. I wish I'd never suggested a birthday balloon; it's more trouble than it's worth.

My stomach's in shreds and I don't feel good about the evening anymore.

I don't know if Tom can sense my feelings or if he's just trying to deal with his own, but he seems to become aggressive and determined.

"I'll get you there, okay?"

"Okay," I say, feeling grateful but ashamed. My brother-in-law is the greatest. Even though he's scared stiff about his child, he still tries to make things right for me.

He presses his foot towards the floor again as the lights change, and I can feel the car accelerate beneath my feet. He's doing 90 miles an hour, with his face set in grim determination. My palms are sweating; I'm scared. I gasp with fear as a car starts to pull out in front of us and Tom swerves to miss it, cussing loudly.

"Tom, slow down," I say, but he shakes his head.

"I want to get back to the hospital..."

Then, as he takes a corner too wide, a truck heads straight for us, and he yanks the steering wheel hard. We soar across the road and the last thing I'm aware of is the sound of my own screaming.

Chapter Two

I don't know where I am. I can hear something but it seems far away. I feel locked inside my head, in darkness. Panic rises inside me as images of the truck coming straight at us filter into my mind. I must be dead. Oh no, it's Becky's birthday. I hear myself moan. Perhaps I'm not dead after all. I try to move my fingers and feel something cool and light covering me. As I try to concentrate, I realize that I can feel my whole body covered in cool linen. Am I alive or dead? I don't know. I try to open my eyes yet they seem stuck. I feel a flash of panic and strain to open my eyelids. I'm blinded and snap them shut again. I try several times again, bearing the blinding light until it no longer sears through me.

I look around. I can't be dead because I'm lying in a hospital bed with a brightly colored flowery curtain pulled around me. As my senses begin to fall into place I lie still, listening. I can hear voices; Becky's here. I moan again.

The curtain is pulled back and a nurse takes my hand.

"How are you feeling, dear?"

I'm hoarse, but croak, "Okay, I think. Where's Becky?"

Becky's face swims before me; she's crying.

"I'm here. Oh Adam..."

She leans over the bed and holds me, and even though my arms are stiff, I hold her, too.

"I'm sorry," I croak, "I messed up your birthday."

"Don't be so silly," she chides, "I'm just glad that you're all right."

She hugs me again and I feel her tears on my cheek.

Mom's standing behind her and she's crying. She leans over and kisses me, and I'm embarrassed. It's years since she's done that. Becky's mom and dad are at the foot of my bed, and suddenly I'm embarrassed with all the attention they're giving me. The nurse comes to my rescue.

"That's enough, now. Let him rest. C'mon, I've got to check his vital signs."

She shoos them away but Becky hangs back for a last kiss.

"I'll see you tomorrow," she says.

"Happy Birthday," I say, feeling bad.

The nurse writes on a clipboard, and as I lie there

behind the curtain listening to the different sounds that belong in a hospital, something slowly dawns on me. Where's Tom?

I feel a sudden jolt of panic and try to sit up, but the nurse puts her hand on my arm and tells me to lie still.

"Where's Tom?" I ask.

"Who?"

"Tom, my brother-in-law. He was driving me to my girlfriend's house. Where is he?"

"Hush, now," she says, "he's not in this hospital. Lie still, I have to get your vital signs."

I lie back, my heart racing.

"Where is he then?"

"Shhh, I don't know. Lie still."

She frowns as she concentrates, and says, "Good, you're doing fine," and then she walks away.

I lie still, listening, my heart racing and my head spinning. Where's Tom? The nurse said that Tom was at a different hospital. I must be at a children's hospital because I'm only sixteen. Tom must be at an adult hospital. My panic subsides.

I fall into a fitful sleep where images of Kelly's bloody leg and racing trucks fire into my dreams and I wake several times covered in sweat. A different nurse comes to see me throughout the night and I mumble, "I know Tom's at a different hospital, but is he all right?"

The nurse writes my vital signs down on her clipboard and says, "Shhh, you'll wake the others."

I didn't realize that there were other people in the room, so I say nothing and determine that I will ask the nurses in the morning when everyone is awake. I need to know that Tom's okay.

It occurs to me how different daytime nurses are than nighttime nurses, for in the morning they bustle into the room, talk loudly as they open the curtains, and gossip about what they did last night. The curtain around my bed is pinned back, showing me the other people in the room. There are two old men coughing into jars and a man who's boasting about his vasectomy. They smile at me.

"You all right, son? How's your head? You looked pretty beat up when they first brought you in. Are you doing okay?"

"Yeah, I suppose so," I say, trying to take everything in.

"Oh good, breakfast," one of the old guys says, as a young man in a uniform pushes a trolley into our room.

I hoist myself up and he gives me eggs and pancakes, and suddenly I'm ravenous. I eat like a thing possessed; I can't remember the last time I ate. When at last I'm full, I sink back into the bed and lie there thinking.

My mind feels foggy, like I can't quite get hold of my thoughts; it's as if they're water slipping through a sieve. They're like a jigsaw puzzle thrown into the air and landing in a thousand different places; it's all there for me to fathom but it's fragmented and incomprehensible. Yet as I'm faced with the same pieces that keep falling in front of me, something vile creeps over me.

If I'm in a children's hospital and Tom's in an adult hospital, how come there are old men in my hospital room? I try to figure it out. Maybe Tom's broken his leg or something and is in another department. But I remember the nurse saying that he isn't in this hospital. My stomach churns with anxiety. Perhaps he was seriously hurt and was taken to another hospital. Yes, that's what must have happened.

I wish I hadn't eaten so much. I feel like I'm going to vomit.

The day drifts past with me being unaware of the time. Mom comes to visit me and brings me candy like I'm a little kid. She fusses around my bed and talks to the other patients in the room.

"Mom," I say, trying to get her attention. "Where's Tom? Is he all right?"

She walks over to one of the old men and re-arranges the flowers next to his bed.

"My, these are pretty," she says, smiling at him.

"Mom," I say louder. "Where's Tom? Is he all right?"

She turns towards me, falters, glances at her watch, and says, "Don't you worry yourself about Tom. Oh, look at the time, I've got to go or I'll be late for work."

She plants a kiss on my forehead and rushes from the room.

My head is reeling. Why won't anyone answer me? Tom must be badly hurt. They know how close we are and they don't want to worry me; that's it.

There's a shift change and the room seems to explode with busyness. Two nurses come in, one bringing fresh pitchers of water and the other bringing fresh towels. I watch everything that's going on and they distract me from my thoughts. The nurses gossip as if we're not there, and one talks about her sister getting a divorce after she found her husband in bed with another woman. They flit about the room, puffing up our pillows and asking how we are without waiting for an answer.

"Excuse me." I cough, but they're too busy. "Excuse me. Can any of you tell me how my brother-in-law, Tom, is doing?"

There's an ominous silence in the room as the nurses glance at each other.

"He's not in this hospital," one nurse says.

"Where is he?" I ask, feeling frustrated.

The nurses look flustered and one says, "I said he's not at this hospital."

They seem to finish what they were doing really quickly and leave. The other men look away and my stomach churns with gnawing anxiety.

I hate the direction my thoughts are heading and, even though I try to think of different explanations for why no one is giving me a straight answer, I come back to the same awful conclusion. I feel a sense of panic creep over me, and despite something inside me searching desperately for another explanation, willing it to chase away the dread that is settling in my soul, there's a cloud of despair banking around me. It's suffocating me as I battle with the inevitable. Is everyone ignoring me because Tom is dead? But just as I think it, a knight inside my head charges forward to rescue me and tells me not to be so silly. Tom's asleep in another hospital, enjoying a night away from Nancy's nagging.

I don't know what's happening to me, for I'm so exhausted, and even though my mind is full of questions and my heart it full of anxiety, I fall asleep, and that's how it is throughout the whole day. I drift into consciousness and then, when my thoughts threaten to overwhelm me, I drift away in unconsciousness, and I hate to admit it, but I'm glad, for something nasty is creeping into my sub-conscious. I long for oblivion, so that I don't have to face my worst fears, so that I don't have to face the truth that I know is sitting in my heart, demanding to be heard.

It's dark outside when I wake up again, and my thoughts surface as I lie still. I can hear muffled voices from beyond the room.

"They should tell him. He's got to know some-time. His mom says that he adores his brother-in-law, and he's been like a father to him. It's not right, they should tell him."

I strain to listen with a sense of foreboding threatening to drown me. I feel vomit rise into my mouth and I swallow; my throat burns, but that's nothing compared to the burning in my eyes. I can feel tears rolling down my face. I cry until my crying turns into sobs, and as I stuff my fist into my mouth to silence myself, my body convulses with pain. Tom's dead.

I don't know how long I cry but it seems to consume me, and when I hear voices coming towards the room, I quickly wipe my eyes and blow my nose in my sheet. Becky walks through the door. She takes one look at my face, which I know has to be red and blotchy, and all but runs towards me.

"Oh, Adam, they told you. Oh, I'm so sorry. I know you were so close."

She sets me off again and she cries with me. I'm embarrassed because I seem to have totally lost control of myself and I don't want her to see me this way, yet I can't stop it. It's humiliating to be crying like a baby in front of my girlfriend, and it adds to my sense of despair. I push her away and turn my back on her.

"Go away and leave me alone," I croak.

"Adam, don't," she says, pulling on my arm.

"GO AWAY!" I yell, my face contorted with pain and humiliation.

I keep my face away from her, as the tears pour down my face and snot rolls down onto my lip. I hear her walk out of the room, crying.

"Hey, son," one of the old men says, "you have a good cry."

"Leave me alone," I snap, turning to face the wall so that I don't have to look at them.

One of the nurses comes in, draws the curtains around me, and sits on the edge of the bed.

She places a hand on my shoulder. "I'm so sorry," she says. "I know you were close."

I can feel anger fire through me.

"You don't know anything. Leave me alone."

"Now honey, I know it feels bad now, but in time you'll feel better," she says.

I look at her, wanting to witness the face of someone who could be so stupid, and I feel unbelievable hatred towards her. I'll never feel any better, never ever. The person I love the most in my life is dead, and he's dead because of me; he was driving too fast because he knew I was upset that we were late. The thoughts cascade upon me, and the pain is unbearable. I can barely breathe as the sobs wrack my body. I'm only vaguely aware of the nurse leaving my bedside and returning with a shot that she drives into my leg.

She pats my shoulder again, and says, "Honey, I'm so sorry, but you really will feel better one day."

I suddenly don't have the energy to tell her to

get lost, and everything in the room seems a blur. The jigsaw in my mind has just exploded and nothing makes any sense anymore, and in a timeless moment the pain has gone and I pray that I've died.

• • • •

My mouth's dry and my eyes are crusted. I feel terrible. The old men are snoring and it's dark outside. I don't know what to do. I can't just lie here with my thoughts, so I try to get out of bed. I hurt but everything seems to be working; no broken bones. I look up and down the corridor outside our room and see a low light at the end, so I head that way.

"Hey, son," a male nurse calls from the opposite direction. "What d'you need?"

I don't know what to say. I don't need anything except Tom, except to turn the clock back...I don't know how many hours. No one can help me.

He walks towards me. "Hi, Adam, I'm Bill. D'you want a drink? Come and sit with me over here." He nods towards the nurse's station bathed in soft light. "It gets a bit lonely here at night."

I follow him and he points to a chair. I sit. He goes to a fridge and hands me a juice.

"Life can be tough, can't it?" he says, handing me a bag of chips, which I refuse.

I can feel tears beginning to prick my eyes again, but this time I'm determined to control them. I clench my teeth and will them to go away, swallowing hard.

I don't know what to say and don't trust myself to speak.

"I lost my uncle when I was about your age. He meant the world to me. It hit me hard."

He becomes quiet, and I don't say anything. It doesn't occur to me that anyone can possibly understand what I'm feeling right this minute, and I don't believe they can.

He stares at the floor and I don't know where to look, so I stare at the wall.

"Grief's a funny thing," he goes on. "Everyone feels it at some point in their lives and yet it feels as if you're the only one that's ever experienced it. You feel utterly alone in it. Man, it's tough."

I still say nothing and we sit there lost in our silence beneath the dim light.

Later, he walks with me back to my bed and I wince as I try to get into it. He stands there and looks at me.

"I'm not going to say 'you'll get over it in time,' because the pain you feel now may always be with you. All I can say to you, having been in your shoes myself, is that it helps to remember the good times you had together. Try to focus on that and not on what you've lost. Listen, grief is one of the hardest things you'll ever have to cope with in life, and although there's no rule book telling you how to get through it, any tip is worth listening to." He pats my arm as he turns to leave. "I wish you well, my friend."

I turn over, and although I expect the tears to fall, my eyes are dry and I can't cry anymore, even though I want to. Crying would be preferable to the awful emptiness inside me, consuming me, yet as my thoughts rob me of sleep, I realize that I'm not empty. I'm filled with guilt. It's my fault that Tom's dead. If I hadn't shown him that I was stressed because we were late to pick up Becky, he wouldn't have driven so fast and he'd still be alive now. Why didn't I call Becky's dad from home so that he could come and get me? I needn't have gone with Tom and Nancy to the hospital. I was too busy thinking of myself and getting to Becky's to think about little Kelly, or that Tom needed to be with her.

I toss and turn, my bruises smarting painfully, but they are nothing compared to the pain in my heart.

If I hadn't been pacing up and down in the emergency room and getting more and more frustrated with the kids charging about, maybe I'd have been able to think. Hell, I could have called a taxi. Okay, it would have cost me money that I don't have to waste, but I could have gotten to Becky's that way, and Tom would still be alive.

Images of his harried face float before me, and they're unbearable. I saw the indecision on his face as he tried to work out what to do; whether to take me to Becky's or stay with Nancy to be there for Kelly's surgery. I know that he saw my frustration and anxiety, and that he acted upon what he saw in my face. I can hardly bear the pain of it all. I should have called Becky's dad. Then Tom would have come out into the reception area to find me, and seeing me gone, he'd have stayed with Nancy and Kelly, and he'd still be alive now. But I was so busy thinking about myself that he felt he had to keep his word to take me to Becky's. His words as he'd been driving too fast come back to me, "I want to get back to the hospital," and my heart feels as if it's in a vice grip. He didn't want to leave the hospital but he felt that he had to, and the only reason he felt that way was because I was stressed out that we were late to pick up Becky.

I hate myself.

I hate the old men snoring. I've never felt hate before and right now, I hate everything and every-body, but most of all, I hate myself. I hate my mom and Nancy, too. Why wouldn't they tell me Tom was dead? Why did they let me find out by overhearing two nurses talking? It's bad enough that he's dead, but to have no one that's willing to tell me the truth is even harder. Right now, I hate them. I hate Becky, too, for she knew but didn't tell me either.

My thoughts are a scattered jigsaw and Becky lies haphazardly among them. Why did it have to be her birthday? If it hadn't been her birthday, none of this would have happened. Why did I have to make such a big deal of her birthday? My friends don't make such a big deal of their girlfriends' birthdays. What's wrong with me that I like to surprise people? If I'd just bought her the locket and not tried to arrange a surprise party, Tom would still be alive. My thoughts sink beneath a sea of despair where I drown. Why did Kelly fall and hurt herself? If she hadn't, Tom would still be alive. I hate myself even more for blaming Kelly, she's just a little kid, and she worships me in the same way that I worship Tom—I mean, worshiped Tom.

Thinking thoughts in past tense is too awful to contemplate, for they confirm the awful truth. The most important person in my life has gone, and I can't see me living in this world without him...I don't know how to. He's been my father, my friend. He's shown me how to be a man. When I think these things, the tears begin to fall again, and my pillow is soaked in seconds. I feel that the very core of me is destroyed and I don't know how to stay alive in this world. It is because of me that the person I care about the most is dead, and although I know that I could never kill myself, I want to be dead. I want the pain to end because it's unbearable.

I sob into my pillow until I have nothing left, and then turn over to lie on my back. The dawn is sending faint shadows across the floor while the old men snore.

Something's happening to me that I don't understand. I know my heart's broken and the guilt will live with me forever, but something's wedging its way into the core of me, something unknown to me, but something that enables me to carry on living, when all I want to do is die and get rid of the pain forever.

If I have to live, then I'll never be happy again. It should be me that's dead, not Tom. It's my fault. I hate God for keeping me alive instead of Tom, and I know that I'll never go to church again.

If I have to live then I'll make sure that my life is a penance for what I did. I can only live if my life is hell, because that's where I should be right now.

The new shift comes on duty. The room suddenly becomes crazy with nurses everywhere. The old men are coughing and I turn away. Something inside me tells me confidently that I won't ever reach their age, to be coughing in some pot; I'll be dead before then. It's my destiny, my path, one I have to take to remain alive, to justify my existence. Yet as I begin to think these thoughts, they flit away and I focus upon the young man pushing the breakfast trolley. I'm starving.

Mom visits me later and I launch into her.

"Why didn't you tell me Tom was dead? How could you? Just when were you planning to tell me? When he failed to come to my graduation?" I don't care that my words hurt her; I want everyone to hurt as much as I'm hurting. She looks flustered and changes the subject.

"Kelly's okay. The surgery was a success, and she'll be okay."

My heart does a double flip as the mention of Kelly takes me back to the emergency room, where Tom made the decision that took him to his death. Thanks Mom. I say nothing.

"Nancy's with her now." I'd wondered why she hadn't been to visit me, but if I were her, I wouldn't want to look at me ever again. I've robbed her of her husband and I've robbed her children of a father.

My mouth's dry, and I wish Mom would leave. I haven't got anything to say to her, and right now I don't think I've got anything left to say to anyone ever again.

"Becky called last night. She said that you were very upset and you told her to go away," Mom says, while she plays with a bunch of flowers that someone has sent me. I don't think I'll ever be able to stand the sight of flowers again. "What's wrong with you? She was only trying to help. You didn't have to bite her head off."

Anger flows through me. How dare my mom speak to me like this when I've just lost the only person I really care about? Right now I don't care about Becky. If it hadn't been for her birthday, Tom would still be alive. I don't care about how Becky feels—it's nothing to me—and what she feels is nothing compared to what I'm feeling.

"Why didn't you tell me, Mom? I heard it from the nurses, whispering like it was some kind of dirty secret."

I can't control myself again, and even though I thought that I was out of tears, they spill down my face again.

"I didn't know what to do. I had Nancy going crazy, what with Kelly's surgery as well, and then there were the boys to take care of, and the twins of course. I didn't know what to do."

She makes me feel like a burden, one extra hassle. All I wanted was the truth and no one would give it to me. I remember the nurses' conversation, "They should tell him, it's not right," and anger sears through me.

"You should have told me. You left me wondering. I...I felt so alone. I felt that everyone knew but me, yet I knew that something was wrong by the way you were acting. You should have told me."

She doesn't have to answer me because a doctor walks into the room. "Ah, I'm glad you're here," he says to Mom, "because Adam can go home. He's a very lucky young man. I hope you know that, young man," he says to me.

I feel a scathing hatred towards him. What does he know? I don't feel lucky at all.

Mom pulls the curtain around me so that I can get dressed. I feel a bit weird. I don't want to stay in the hospital listening to the old men coughing up phlegm and snoring throughout the night, but the thought of going back to my life that can never be the same again fills me with dread.

I get dressed slowly, wincing as my body hurts.

The old men wish me luck as I leave, and I don't know what to say, so I mumble, "Thanks," even though I don't mean it. I follow Mom outside.

As we drive along the roads that I know so well, everything looks different. I feel as if I've never seen any of it before, even though I know these roads like the back of my hand. I feel as if my world has slipped off its axis and everything is slightly off center. As Mom pulls into the drive, I feel really nauseous.

Even though I don't want to go inside because I know that everything in our house will remind me of Tom, I follow her, my stomach churning and my mouth dry.

The boys rush over to me, and they suddenly look older. They look at me as if I've grown another head. My heart feels so heavy that I can't even smile at them. They leave my side and go back to flop in front of the television. Jed stands there not knowing what to say.

Nancy stands in the doorway and our eyes meet. Something flashes between us; she starts to cry and walks away. My heart is crushed; she blames me, I know she does. I've just seen it in her eyes.

Chapter Three

The look on Nancy's face is too much to bear, so I go straight to my room and slam the door. Mom comes up after a while. She doesn't knock.

"Dinner's ready, come downstairs."

"I'm not hungry," I snap. The way I feel right this minute I doubt that the lump in my throat will ever allow me to eat again.

"Adam, you've got to eat something," Mom pleads.

"I'm not hungry," I say, and she turns around and heads for the door. "There's no need to be rude," she says, "you're not the only one hurting, y'know."

I clench my teeth until my jaw hurts. No, I know that. I know that my sister and nieces are hurting, too. After all, thanks to me, Nancy's lost her husband and the girls have lost their dad. Thanks for reminding me, Mom.

Jed comes up and sits awkwardly on my bed.

"Mom's throwing a hissy fit downstairs because you won't come down."

"I don't care," I say, as I turn over to face the wall. "Leave me alone."

The bed shifts as he stands up. He sighs and leaves the room.

I must have fallen asleep because the room is dark as I become aware of knocking on my door. I don't answer.

There's a chink of light as it opens.

"Adam," Becky says gently. "Adam, are you awake?"

"I am now," I say moodily.

"I brought you a sandwich," she says, flipping on the light.

"I don't want anything."

"Well, I'll just leave it here, okay?"

There's something about her voice and the way she moves that's alien and not a bit like the Becky I know. It riles me. She's trying too hard. Why can't everyone just leave me alone? Don't they know that they make things worse? I've got nothing to say to anyone because when they talk to me they seem to want something back, and I've got nothing left inside me other than guilt and pain. The look on their faces, demanding that I make them feel better, adds to the guilt and loneliness in my heart.

Becky puts the sandwich down and sits on the

edge of my bed. Her voice sounds shaky.

"If you'd just talk about it..." she starts to say.

"What's there to say?" I snap.

I ignore the tear rolling down her cheek.

"Adam," she wails, "please don't shut me out. Don't you love me anymore?"

I look at her, and at once my heart feels hard. She's thinking about us, when the most important person in my life has gone. Suddenly she makes me sick, and as my grief rises within me, I can't believe that just a few days ago I thought that she was the most important person in my life. The thought is a betrayal to Tom and I feel anger course through me.

"If I wasn't coming to pick you up for your stupid birthday, none of this would have happened."

Tears are pouring down her face now and she looks horrified, but I don't care. I feel some relief at having someone to unload my grief on, for it's suffocating me, and I feel a cruel sense of release as she runs from the room, sobbing.

Moments later Mom comes bursting through the door.

"What did you say to Becky? She's really upset. What's the matter with you?" she says, looking angry and exasperated at the same time.

"Go away," is all I can think of to say.

When I've eaten the sandwich, I stare up at the ceiling, willing my thoughts to focus on the fan going round and round, anything other than Tom and the emptiness I feel.

The only time I leave my room over the next few days is to go to the bathroom and get something to eat. I brush the boys aside when they beg me to make pancakes, and their hurt faces are nothing compared to the hurt inside me. I long for the oblivion of sleep but I fear it, too, as each time I drift off Tom's face floats before me and again I see his indecision as to whether to stay at the hospital or drive me to Becky's house.

I creep downstairs in the middle of the night and pour myself a large glass of Mom's whiskey. It tastes foul and burns my throat, but within a short time I'm asleep, and I don't seem to remember my dreams in the morning.

It's the day of the funeral and I'm torn in two. I want to refuse to go but I can't because that would be disrespectful towards Tom. Mom nags me to take a shower, and I realize that the last time I showered was two hours before Tom died.

I'm so anxious that I have to use the bathroom over and over. Mom's dressed in black and looks more like she's about to go clubbing than to a funeral. She keeps checking her hair in front of the mirror and I hate her for being so shallow. She's shouting at the boys to stop jumping on the furniture, and is telling them to get ready, when Sherrie walks through the door.

"Aren't you ready yet?" she says, glancing around, and then her eyes rest on me. "Adam, you're not going looking like that, are you? Do your hair."

I mutter something foul under my breath as I walk past her, and I sit outside waiting for them all to get ready. I'm surprised that Nancy's not here. In fact, come to think of it, she hasn't been at our house since the day I came home from the hospital.

Sherrie's new boyfriend, Jason, comes outside and sits on the wall next to me.

"It's a bit hectic in there," he says, pulling out a packet of cigarettes and lighting one.

"Can I have one?" I ask.

"I didn't know you smoked," he says, handing me one and flicking his lighter under my nose.

I don't tell him that I've never smoked before in my life and until now have always been determined not to, as my granddad died of lung cancer, but now I don't care if I die of lung cancer, in fact it would be preferable to living without Tom.

I feel a wave of nausea wash over me as I suck on the end of the cigarette, and will the dizziness to go away. I don't want him to know that this is the first time I've smoked, so I focus upon battling the nausea, and it helps me to channel my thoughts away from Tom's funeral.

By the time I've finished the cigarette Mom and the boys are finally ready, and she picks on them as they climb into the car. Sherrie rolls her eyes and shakes her head, then orders Jed to go with Mom.

"Adam, you're coming with us, and do something with your hair, will you?"

My head is swimming and I'm still trying not to throw up, so I don't have the energy to argue with her. I sit in the back of their car, hanging on to the seat in front of me, hoping to steady myself. The motion of the car makes it worse, and by the time we get to the church I barely make it outside the car before I vomit everywhere. Sherrie shouts at me and tells me that I'm embarrassing her.

I'm so humiliated, especially when Tom's dad comes over to me and says, "Don't worry, son, I know you and Tom were really close. Grief gets you that way sometimes. Here..." and he hands me a tissue.

I feel ashamed that he should attribute my vomiting to grief when it's because I've just smoked my first cigarette.

Nancy's dressed in black and I swear that I'm not imagining it, but she barely meets my eye. She's crying before we go into the church and Mom puts her arm around her, while Sherrie sniffs with disapproval. She corrals the boys and herds them to their seats. I follow behind, my stomach in shreds. I'd give anything to be somewhere else, and I'd also give anything for some of Mom's whiskey...I just want out of here. My hands are trembling.

I hear a familiar cough and turn around. Becky's sitting between her mom and dad. Her parents smile at me but she stares ahead. I turn around and face the front.

The organist starts to play a somber piece of music, and everyone stands; so do I. Jed and the boys turn around, and the look on their faces makes me turn around, too.

Six men dressed in black are walking very slowly with a white coffin propped on their shoulders. I know I gasp out loud. This can't be happening. I feel faint and so sick that I long to vomit again, even though I've got nothing left inside me. Sherrie shoots me a warning look and I hate her for not knowing how I'm feeling, and for not caring. She just cares about what things look like.

I don't know how I get through the service—the hymns, the readings, and some guy talking about Tom who obviously didn't know him. No one who hadn't been fishing with Tom could possibly know him as I did. I hate their shallow words and wonder if they're being paid to hold this service. My jaw hurts from clenching my teeth in an attempt to hold back the tears. I can hear Nancy crying a few rows in front of me and Jed sniffs occasionally. I'm not going to cry; I refuse to. I can't. I'm afraid to, for if I start I fear that I may never stop.

I long for another cigarette, for even though it made me vomit, it forced me to focus on something else, and I'm desperate not to think about the scene in front of me.

I can hear Becky crying and I feel angry towards her. Why's she crying? Tom was nothing to her.

Tom's mom is crying so loudly that the hairs on the back of my neck stand up, and I long for it to be over, but it seems to go on and on forever. We sit down, then stand up and sing, then we kneel down and everyone says "Amen" several times before we sit and then stand again. The boys are fidgeting and Mom hisses at them. Nancy blows her nose yet again and adds another tissue to the pile on the chair next to her.

Kelly and the twins aren't here; I guess Nancy thinks they're too young to go to a funeral. I think maybe I'm too young to go to a funeral. I hate it, not only because it's boring and seems to have nothing to do with Tom, but because it forces unbearable thoughts upon me. The person I love the most in my life is cold and lifeless in that pretty white box in front of me, and it fills me with horror.

There's a huge clap of thunder and the heavens open, and I hear Sherrie whisper that her new suit is going to get wet.

The organist seems to be playing louder in order for us to hear over the thunder, and the music seems to change. Suddenly the six men dressed in black stand and position themselves around Tom's coffin. When one man nods they bob down, position it on their shoulders, and stand together. They shuffle around so that Tom leaves the church feet first. Mom urges Nancy to follow with Tom's parents and then hisses at the boys to keep up with her.

I follow Sherrie, and my legs feel weak. We file out of the church and follow the men carrying Tom towards a large, deep hole in the ground. The rain is coming down in sheets, and many people have umbrellas and are huddled together, sheltering, even though the force of the rain splashes mud onto their legs. I don't want to be near anyone, so I stand alone, staring into the black hole that's going to hold my Tom forever more. There's a massive puddle of water at the bottom and the sides of the hole look as if they're about to cave in. A bizarre thought crosses my mind, "Tom's going to get wet and won't be able to get dry. He'll be wet for all eternity." I shiver involuntarily at the thought, and as the six men begin to lower the coffin into the drenched hole in the ground, Tom's mom and Nancy howl.

The rain pounds upon every part of me, and my hair is plastered to my face. Becky's parents call softly to me to shelter myself under their umbrella but I shake my head. I want to be uncomfortable; I want to hurt. Tom doesn't deserve to spend the rest of eternity in a soaked dark hole in the ground, so I don't deserve to be comfortable. My life's no longer mine, it's a penance for what I did, and every time I'm uncomfortable or hurting I will know that I'm paying for Tom's death.

The rain beats down on me and it rolls down my

neck and inside my shirt, chilling me to the bone.

Everyone around me is crying. The boys hold Jed's hands and Nancy is in pieces. Mom's doing her best to comfort her but every so often I see her pat her hair and frown, and I'm sure she's not thinking about losing Tom.

Becky's dad steps forward with a box and opens it. There are loads of red roses inside and he nods at me.

"Take one, son. Throw it in his grave as a sign of how much you loved him."

Suddenly there's a huge lump in my throat. I take one and momentarily stare at it, as raindrops cling to the velvet petals. I step up to the grave and look down. Tom's white coffin is splattered in mud, and it seems awful to me that not only is he dead and has to lie soaked to the skin for all eternity, but his beautiful white coffin is now ruined by rain and mud. I feel as if I've slipped into a horror movie, one that I can't escape from. I pray that I'll hear knocking sounds from inside the coffin telling us that we got it all wrong; Tom's alive after all. We just have to help him out of the hole that's filling up with water as we stand around it, and then we can go home and joke about it...Tom and me, always joking, always together.

The water continues to rise around the coffin and I throw my rose in. I'm so horrified that something powerful comes over me, and I have a hard time not throwing myself in after him. I'm desperate to be dead, and yet my beliefs won't allow me to kill myself. I'm stuck in a place where there's no relief, a place where I can't hide from myself or what I did.

As the rose hits the coffin and begins to float in the rising water, I can't stand it anymore and I bolt, skidding, as I try to run on the muddy ground. I don't know where I'm going; all I know is that I have to get away from here, and I hate myself as it happens, but I begin to sob.

There's a forest nearby and so I head for it, crashing through the bushes until I'm deep within it. My chest hurts as I gasp for air, my sobs competing with the need to breathe.

I sit on a fallen log trying to catch my breath as my sobs echo around the trees. The daylight is shut out, barred by the canopy of trees above my head. Even though I know it's raining really hard, barely any rain reaches the forest floor. As my breath begins to slow, I notice a rabbit nibbling on the plants by my feet. It seems totally unconcerned about me and my ragged breath. I can't believe that it's not frightened of me. I sit still and wonder if rabbits have feelings. If they don't, I'd gladly change places with it, for I feel as if I'm a seething mass of feelings without form. I seem to have lost my sense of self, of knowing who I am; I feel as if I'm nobody without Tom in my life.

I have no idea how long I've been sitting in the woods, unable to cry anymore and with snot on my shirtsleeve. The rabbit has long since become bored with me and hopped away. It feels late as the dim light fades. I stand up wearily, my ass sore, and even though my soul feels homeless, I go home.

There are several cars outside our house and all the lights are on. I slip in through the door and head for my room but get half way up the stairs when Mom catches me.

"Have you been stealing my whiskey?" she demands. "Don't lie, I know it has to be you. Have you any idea how embarrassing it was to invite people back to the house and then find that I hadn't anything to offer them?"

Sherrie stands behind her and pipes in, never missing the opportunity to pick on me.

"And that's not all. Jason says that he's smoking, too."

"What! Since when?"

Anger sparks through me when I see the smirk on Sherrie's face. I want to claw her eyes out. How could she be so hateful when my whole world has fallen to pieces? I say something foul to her and turn my back on them both.

"Are you going to let him speak to me that way?" Sherrie says to Mom.

"Come back down here," Mom shouts, sounding slightly drunk.

I say the same thing to Mom; I really don't care anymore. I don't care about anything or anyone anymore. I feel as if something inside me has died alongside Tom. I throw myself on my bed and moments later the door opens. It's Becky.

"What're you doing here?" I ask her, surprised that she's here.

"I was worried about you. We didn't know where you'd gone. Your mom asked us to come back, and I couldn't go until I knew you were all right. I forgive you for being mean to me the other night."

I look at her and I want to laugh. She forgives me. Something really vile seems to bubble up inside me, something that has nowhere to go other than towards her.

"You forgive me, do you? Well, that's great. Thank you," I say, with sarcasm dripping from me. My face contorts with pain. "Do you really think that I care whether you forgive me for being mean? You think I was being mean? I don't think so, this is being mean..." Something horrible seems to take over me and I thrust my face into hers.

"This is being mean...It's your fault that Tom's dead. If he hadn't been driving so fast to come and pick you up for your stupid birthday, he'd still be alive. You're the reason he's dead."

I'm so mad that spit flies from my mouth and lands on her. She pushes me away and cries, "I hate you," as she runs from my room.

"That's fine, because I hate you, too," I shout after her.

My heart's racing so fast that I flop down onto my bed, feeling faint.

How dare she say that she forgives me? Can't she see how much pain I'm in? Does the world revolve around her and what she feels?

My heart's still racing minutes later when the door opens again, but this time it's Becky's dad.

"Can I come in?"

He doesn't wait for me to answer, but closes the door behind him, and sits on the edge of my bed.

"Son, I know you're hurting at the moment, but don't push the people who love you away. You're a good kid and I really like you. If I didn't, I'd whoop your ass for saying what you've just said to Becky, but I understand that you're upset, so I'll let it go. You need to talk to someone about how you feel, and I'm always here for you if you want to talk, okay?"

He makes me feel vaguely ashamed of myself, but I chase the feeling away. I feel bad enough without making it worse. I don't know what to say so I turn over and face my wall, knowing that I'm being rude, but I just can't help it. I really feel as if something inside me has died, and it's beyond me to care about anything anymore. He sits there for a moment longer and then stands.

"Okay, I understand that you're upset. Call me if you need someone to talk to, and if it's not me, then talk to someone, because you need to. Grief is one of the hardest things you'll ever have to deal with in life, and we all need help to get through it. I know I did when my brother died in Vietnam."

I continue to stare at the wall, remaining motionless as his words trigger memories of the male nurse's comments in the hospital, and I only move when I hear him close my door.

I strain to listen as Becky and her parents leave the house, rev their car and drive away. Good, I'm glad they've gone. The sight of Becky is too raw. She reminds me that she's the reason we were in the car on the night Tom died, and as I'm consumed by blame and am desperate to lay it at the feet of someone other than me, I know that I'll never be able to look at her again.

I sit up, reassured that they've gone, and I strip my walls of all her photos. Slowly, with deliberation, I tear them into shreds before dropping them into the trashcan.

I hear footsteps on the stairs and instinct tells me that they're heading towards my door. I'm not wrong. My door bursts open and Mom looks furious. Behind her is Sherrie with a vague smirk on her face.

"What are you doing?" Mom shouts at me. "How could you act that way towards Becky and her dad? You make me sick. You haven't said one word to Nancy, and she's hurting more than you are. How can you be so selfish? She's downstairs in pieces, trying to take care of Kelly and the twins and you haven't given her a thought, have you? You selfish little..."

She cusses at me.

Sherrie joins in and I'm aware that she seems to be enjoying herself. "I can't believe how much you embarrassed us today. First, you go and throw up everywhere; you could have asked Jason to stop before we got to the church. Then you refuse to stand with anyone at the grave, and *then* you run off and worry everyone to death. How selfish is that?"

My head is spinning, not only with pain but also with anger, yet everything they've said is true, so I don't know how to respond. They seem to take my silence as an apology and their voices drop.

Mom says, "Get yourself downstairs and talk to your sister. It's her husband that's dead. She's the one that should be in pieces, not you. Think of some-one else for a change. Oh, and you can do chores to pay me back for stealing my whiskey."

They leave.

I lie on my bed, with my heart hammering. Some-thing feels really wrong. My conscience flickers like a flame in a draught. I know I've been miserable and snappy, but can't anyone see the pain I'm in? It isn't only Nancy's pain, it's mine, too; it's not a competi-tion to see who's in the most pain. Yet the thought of Kelly being downstairs, still with stitches in her leg, forces me to do as Mom asks. I feel shamed into going downstairs and joining the others, and mixed with my shame is anger and anxiety. The only good thing is that Becky and her parents have gone.

I barely get to the bottom of the stairs when Kelly scoots across the floor on her ass, her leg heavily bandaged. She smiles at me. She's too young to know what's happened, too young to know that I'm responsible for her father's death. Although I've just blamed Becky for Tom's death, I know deep down that it's a lie; I'm the one to blame, it's my fault that he's dead, not hers.

The faith in Kelly's eyes is both comforting and yet devastating, and it strips me naked. I pick her up, being careful to avoid her bandaged leg, and suddenly I want to cry. There's something so non-judgmental in her eyes. She doesn't understand. All I see in her is love for me, and I've never noticed this before, but she looks just like Tom. I hug her tight and she starts to struggle to be free. I put her down as I enter the family room. Everyone turns to look at me.

I look at Nancy. Her face is blotchy red, and I know that she's been crying all day. The twins are crawling all over her, trying to get her attention, but she seems stiff and distant. They cry and whine.

I feel awkward and don't know what to do or what to say. Jason comes to my rescue and I'm grateful.

"Hey, man, let's go outside."

I follow him, and we sit in the backyard, idly watching the boys on the swing set, hooting and hollering to each other, and then demanding that we watch them hang by their bent knees.

Jason talks as he offers me a cigarette, and I suck hard as he holds the lighter to its tip. It glows in the darkness. I exhale, and although my head starts to swim immediately, I suck on it again. I'm oblivious to what the boys are doing and only focus on controlling the nausea I know is going to come.

We sit in silence for a moment and then he says, "Rough day."

I nod.

"You okay?"

I shrug. I don't want to talk to him about how I feel; he can't take Tom's place.

We go back into the house as it starts to rain, and I follow Jason into the kitchen where he pours me a soda and laces it with vodka. Sherrie would kill him if she knew, but I'm not telling and neither is Jason.

We sit on the sofa, and Jason gets up twice to fill our glasses. I'm beginning to feel numb and a bit sick, but the edges of my pain are beginning to blur. Nancy and I are engaged in a weird kind of dance, where neither of us looks directly at the other but just catches the tail end of a glance, our eyes locking for a fraction of a second before looking in the opposite direction. I just don't know what to say to her, and the sight of her red eyes tears me in two.

Kelly scoots over to sit on my lap and I'm relieved to have someone to focus on, rather than trying to avoid Nancy's veiled glances at me. I feel false, though, for my heart's not into playing with Kelly. I feel as much guilt when I look at Kelly as I do when I look at Nancy's tearful face.

Nancy makes a noise that's a cross between a cough and a sob, and we all look at her. Her face is contorted. In the split second it takes for her to draw a breath, I can't tell if her face is contorted with pain or anger, and I don't get the time to work it out before she starts screaming at me.

"Oh, so *now* you care about Kelly, do you? It's a shame you didn't care about her the night she hurt her leg. If you'd cared about anyone other than yourself, my Tom would still be alive. All this is your fault. He should've been at the hospital with Kelly, but no, you had to drag him off to go and pick up your precious Becky, didn't you?"

She sounds like a crazy person and the girls start crying. My head is spinning and I'm desperate to get out of here, but little Kelly is still sitting in my lap, looking frightened. I can't move. Suddenly everything seems as if it's in slow motion; there's shock on everyone's faces, and no one knows what to do. Nancy pushes the twins off her roughly, and they fall to the floor as she lunges across the room at me, her hands slapping wildly. I can't move because of Kelly. I want to push her aside and get out of here, but I can't because of her leg, and because she'd be even more frightened than she is now. It seems as if Nancy has forgotten Kelly's leg because she slaps at me across Kelly, screaming that it's all my fault.

Sherrie looks stunned. Jason, his breath thick with alcohol and cigarettes, scoops Kelly, who's now screaming, from my lap and moves away. At last I can defend myself, but something stops me. I sit there and let Nancy slap the hell out of me because I know I deserve it. It hurts, but it's nothing compared to the pain inside me. I let all the hateful things she says soak into me, because all of them are true. I did this. It's my fault that Tom's dead, my fault that she has no husband and my fault that the girls have no father.

I'm only vaguely aware of her being pulled off me, her eyes wild and crazy, and I feel as if I'm watching it all from deep within me, a place far away. I stand up, my own face painfully contorted, and there's only one thing that drives me. I have to get away from here, away from Nancy and the girls, and away from myself.

Chapter Four

I blunder my way out of the family room, pushing aside the boys, who are silent for once, and with no rational thought in my head, I head through the kitchen. I see Mom's car keys sitting on the table and I take them. I have to get away. My head's spinning. I have no plan. I just need to get as far away as I can from here and Nancy's cutting words.

I still have Tom's voice in my head as I start the car, "Check the mirror before pulling away," and as I check it, I see Mom and Sherrie running out of the house towards the car. I put my foot down, and when I glance at the mirror, they are in the distance. I screech around the corner, feeling the back end of the car slide across the road. I don't care. I want to be dead so that I can be with Tom. The pain of living without him is just too great.

I'm vaguely aware that tears are rolling down my face, which sting as they roll over the raw places on my cheeks where Nancy has just battered me. I'm glad of the pain, though, because the more pain I feel, the better my penance, for everything she said was true. It *is* my fault that Tom's dead, that she doesn't have a husband and the girls don't have a father. It's also true that I'm selfish and that I put myself first that night. There's no argument inside me to soften her words because they're all true.

I'm downtown and have no recollection of getting here; I've been locked inside my head with Nancy's words damning me. My body seems to have been driving the car, not me. By the time I realize where I am, I can't cry anymore. I wipe my eyes with my fingers and my nose on my sleeve, and slow the car down.

Every so often a police car drives past but doesn't seem to take any notice of me. Somewhere deep in my mind I realize that Mom can't have reported me to the police for taking her car, because if she had, I'd have been stopped by now. I cruise around, going everywhere and going nowhere.

I pull over and within seconds a woman comes over to me.

"Hey, how'ya doin'?"

I want to tell her to get lost because I want to be alone, but she offers me a cigarette and I take it. She crouches down, leaning forward, and as she holds her lighter out for me, my eyes fall upon her breasts, which are barely covered—and huge.

"What's the matter, baby? You look like you could do with some lovin'. D'you want to see what mama's got for you?"

I don't know what to say; my head's swimming from all the alcohol Jason gave me. She opens the car door and pulls on my arm.

"C'mon, come with me."

I allow her to lead me. I feel really sick from smoking and drinking too much alcohol. I'm barely aware of where she takes me, since it's dark, but she holds my hand tightly.

When she finally turns on a light, I look around a shabby room. She pulls at my clothes and I let her. There's a defiance within me that argues inside my brain. Tom is dead—he can never feel anything again—and if I have to live, then everything I feel, I'll feel for him. So even though I know what she is and that I shouldn't be here doing this, I let her unzip my jeans, and my body responds to her as she pulls me down onto a dirty bed in the corner of the room.

Afterwards she pours me a drink.

"Your first time?" she asks knowingly, and of course I lie.

"Of course not. I've had loads of girls."

"Yes, honey," she purrs, running her finger down my chest.

Despite my brain being numbed by grief and alcohol, something seems to click into place and I look at her as if for the first time.

Her lipstick is smudged and so is her heavy black eye makeup. I feel sick; she's disgusting. She's old, horrible and haggard, and she must be older than my mom.

I jump up.

"Hey, baby, what's the matter? Come back, don't you want some more?"

I pull my clothes on, desperate to get away from her and my shame. She seems angry and demands money. I've only got ten dollars on me and throw it at her, before running out of the room.

My hands are shaking as I fumble to open the car door, and I turn the car radio up to smother the memories in my head of her moaning and grunting. I drive down the street but have to stop as her smell, which seems to hover around me, makes me throw up.

I can't remember getting home, I just remember creeping into the house. All the cars have gone and the house is in darkness. My head's spinning with everything that's happened today. It's been awful, that's the only thing I can say about it. I feel so empty. I also feel ashamed. If Tom were here, I know that he wouldn't have let me smoke, he wouldn't have given me alcohol, and I know that he would've been disgusted at what I've just done. I wanted to make love to Becky, not some old woman that's older than my mom, a person that doesn't even know my name or care about me in any way.

I'm just about to put my foot on the first step when Mom stands in the family room doorway in the darkness. She makes me jump. She looks odd, and I'm surprised when she doesn't shout at me. I put the light on. She looks as if she's been crying.

"Are you all right, Adam? Nancy shouldn't have gone off on you like that," she shakes her head. "After you left, she went at me, too."

I notice that she's got red marks on her face.

"She went crazy...said it was my fault that Tom was dead because if I had cleaned up the garden there wouldn't have been any glass there for Kelly to cut herself on."

She catches her breath, and sobs, "She's right, of course. If Kelly hadn't fallen on the trash in the back yard, Tom wouldn't have driven so fast and he wouldn't have been killed..."

She looks defeated, and suddenly I feel sorry for her. I know just how she's feeling, and so I put my arms around her. She doesn't look so hard anymore, and her anger at me for stealing her whiskey seems to have gone.

She finally breaks away, sniffing, and I follow her into the family room. She's made up the sofa bed.

"Who's staying over?" I ask.

She pours two glasses of whiskey and hands me one. I try not to look surprised or pleased. Her crying increases.

"It was awful. Nancy completely lost it. Sherrie

had to pull her off me. The kids were terrified. I've never seen her like that. She looked totally crazy. She was screaming about things that happened years ago, things I'd forgotten, but obviously she hadn't."

"What did she say?" I ask intrigued.

She shakes her head as tears flow down her face. "That I was a terrible mother and I had never stuck up for her. She said that I'd favored you and Sherrie. She sounded like she hated me. She said that you were my favorite child, and that I'd ruined you and made you selfish."

I don't know what to say. I don't see how anyone could say that I'm my mom's favorite because she nags me to death.

"Then she started on Sherrie, and she was screaming like a crazy person. Sherrie slapped her and screamed back." She shook her head. "Those poor kids, they were terrified. Jason called the police and they took her away."

I'm shocked and take a gulp of the whiskey that burns my throat as it goes down. Mom wipes her eyes with a tissue and blows her nose.

"They took her to a psychiatric hospital. The kids are upstairs in my bed. It took me ages to settle them down."

She drains her drink and pours another.

"Where have you been?"

I hope my face doesn't betray me, as I feel it burn.

"Oh, nowhere. I just drove around. I had to get out. Sorry."

She grabs my hand and shakes her head.

"I don't blame you, but you shouldn't have taken my car, as you haven't passed your test. You'd have been in trouble if the police had stopped you."

That's all she says and I'm surprised. I'd expected her to go crazy at me, but there's something about her that seems defeated. She stands up and tells me to go to bed and get some sleep because the babies will be awake early.

"I need you to baby sit tomorrow," she says. "I've got to go to work."

I can't tell her that I don't want to, because she looks so awful. I climb the stairs and go to the bathroom, and even though it's late, and everyone's asleep, I take a shower because I feel so dirty. I scrub myself, chasing my feelings of shame away.

It seems as if morning is here as soon as my head hits the pillow, and I can hear the babies crying and the boys fighting. Mom's shouting as she opens my door; the gentleness I saw in her last night is gone.

"Get up, Adam. I'm going to be late; my ride will be here in a minute. Get up, the babies need changing."

I groan. My mouth's dry and tastes like the bottom of a bird cage. No one told me that drinking alcohol gives you a hangover that feels like hell. I stretch and long to go back to sleep, but just then Kelly walks up to my bed and shakes me.

"Uncle Adam, make me pancakes."

I open my eyes and there she is, the image of Tom, and my stomach does a double flip. I sit up and she clambers onto my bed.

"Mommy was naughty. The policeman took her away to be with Daddy."

I feel goose bumps prickle my skin. She's so little and doesn't understand anything.

"Was Daddy naughty, too? When's Mommy and Daddy coming home?"

I don't know what to say; it's too hard. I get out of bed with my head throbbing, saying, "C'mon, let's go and make pancakes."

She seems to forget her questions immediately and a stray thought wanders into my head. *I wish I were three years old and satisfied by a pancake.*

My head throbs as Mom flies out of the house, planting a kiss on my cheek, something she's never done before. She tells me to take care of the kids and that she'll bring pizza home for dinner.

I drink several glasses of water—for my thirst is like a sponge—and battle against the irritation I feel as the babies cry. They both need changing and the smell turns my stomach, but I push on to get it done, feeling resentful. The boys get up and demand pancakes. I snap at them and then feel guilty. I shout up the stairs to Jed and tell him he's lazy and to get downstairs now and help me. I've got five little kids to look after and he's still in bed. It's not fair.

Eventually he strolls into the kitchen; I bark at him, and he snaps back at me. The boys act out and the babies cry, feeling the tension in the air. My temper rises as the noise builds. My nerves feel taut, as if they're going to snap and fly across the room, slashing everyone in front of me, and Kelly starts crying. I pick her up and hold her tightly, willing myself to calm down.

"I want my Daddy," she cries, and her words slice through my heart, and tears prick my eyes. I put her down and she cries alongside the babies.

"I can't do this," I say to Jed, "you do it."

"Hey!" he shouts, as I run from the kitchen.

I know I can't leave because he's too young to be left with five little kids, so I sit outside on the wall and I hate myself as I cry.

I don't know how many minutes pass before I take a deep breath and go back into the house, my feelings safely locked away. I've decided that the only way to cope is to feel nothing.

The boys are being awful and I catch Jed slapping them.

"Hey, stop," I shout, and he cusses at me as he leaves the house. I'm on my own. I tell the boys that I'll give them candy if they each hold one of the twins and feed them. Suddenly they're motivated and stop whining. They pick up the babies and stagger with them in their arms over to the sofa, feeding them cereal. The noise level drops immediately and so I calm down a bit.

Kelly looks up at me, her eyes glistening.

Before she can ask me any questions that threaten to destroy me, I say, "Okay, let's make these pancakes, shall we?"

She smiles at me, her questions forgotten, and I try to keep her busy so that she and I don't focus upon the one person that's never going to come back into our lives.

The boys, who'll do anything for the promise of candy, feed the twins dry cereal, which takes them ages to eat, and while they're quiet I make pancake after pancake, my thoughts chased away as the mixture spreads across the frying pan and blue smoke hovers above the cooker. Kelly laughs as I toss the pancakes, and, hearing her, the boys put the twins down and come out into the kitchen to see what she's laughing at.

They egg me on. "Toss them higher, Adam, go on, higher."

"Okay," I say, almost as if it's someone else speaking, for I really don't want to do this. I want to be in the forest away from everyone, to be alone with my grief and guilt. But with five expectant faces before me and no one to help, I bury my feelings and act as if I'm someone else without a care in the world.

"Okay, watch out, here we go."

I position the frying pan in front of me and in a flash the pancake rises into the air, flips over and lands back into the pan. The boys cheer, and Kelly joins in. The twins rock and giggle on the kitchen floor.

"More, more," Kelly says, and so I begin a production line, and I've no idea how long I spend feeding and entertaining the kids. There's mess everywhere, especially as I missed one pancake and it landed on the floor, and another landed in the sink, but I don't care because the kids are laughing and they're happy. And all the time they're happy, Kelly won't ask me where Tom is.

The door opens and Sherrie stands there with her hands on her hips.

"What on earth is going on?" she shouts above the children's laughter. Jed stands behind her. "Why have you been picking on Jed?" she demands.

Instantly anger flashes through me. He's done nothing to help me and yet she picks on me, not him. I slam the frying pan down with a half-cooked pancake in it and shout at Sherrie.

"You take care of them, if you're so smart."

Kelly's face switches from laughter to anxiety, and she cries out as I head for the door.

"Uncle Adam, don't go." She bursts into tears and howls, "I want my Daddy."

My heart feels as if it's being ripped in two as I slam the door behind me.

I get in Mom's car and drive away. My mind's reeling. How can my life have changed so much in just a couple of weeks? I've lost the most important person to me, been blamed for his death, and done things that I wouldn't have dreamed of doing if Tom had still been alive. My mom can't cope and leaves everything to me, and then there's Sherrie who never misses the opportunity to dump her hatred onto anyone around her. I can't take any more. I wish I'd died with Tom, for living with the guilt is so painful that I don't know what to do. My sister's in a mental hospital, her kids cry for their dad, and the look on their faces as they love me feels like the ultimate betrayal; it's my fault they have no father. I don't deserve the love they show me, and I don't deserve to live.

I have no recollection of driving into town. My jaw aches as my teeth are clenched in pain. I feel like I'm a puppet, moving as if someone is pulling my strings, making me do things that I wouldn't normally do. I'm totally numb, and I don't care where I'm going or what I'm doing, I'm so saturated in grief that I just don't care about anything. Life without Tom is a living hell and somewhere deep within me I make a wish, one that will grant me a hasty exit from this life, so that my pain will stop.

My body is numb with pain as I climb the steps to the old woman's bedroom. I don't know why I'm here—I don't want to be. But something forces me to climb the steps, and as I do, I feel even more like a puppet.

My hand—it feels as if it doesn't belong to me—knocks on the door.

I can hear someone inside.

"Hang on," she says.

I wait and eventually she opens the door. She smiles at me.

"Well, honey, you wanted some more after all. C'mon in."

I ignore her smile, which highlights the lines around her mouth and eyes, and step into the dingy room, looking around me.

It smells of cheap perfume and a smell that I can't quite place. She takes my jacket and sidles up to me, running her hand around my neck, pulling my face towards hers. I shut my eyes, not wanting the image of her face in my head, but as she kisses me, something starts to happen to my body. I begin to feel alive...more alive than I've felt since Tom died.

I'm sober this time and so everything she does to me lodges in my brain. I can't blame alcohol for my being here this time, and as she works over my body, I have to accept a reality: Since Tom died, all I've felt is pain, yet as she does what she's paid to do, I actually feel *something*, something other than pain.

Over the next few weeks I steal money from Mom's and Sherrie's purses and visit her as often as

I can, and it feels good. I've become addicted to the feelings she forces my body to feel, for the only time my pain seems to subside is when I'm having sex with her. She distracts me from my pain. Yet in the moments when I'm alone in my room, guilt swamps me and I feel that I've sold my soul to the devil; but even as the shame settles over me I know that I deserve no better. It's my fault that Tom died and I have to pay for it for the rest of my life.

I become proficient at lying to Mom and Sherrie, who accuse me of stealing, and my throat becomes hoarse from shouting at them. Jed and I fight as I blame him for taking the money. He blackens my eye, and we roll about on the floor punching each other. Even though my face smarts, it feels good to let my anger out. When Jason pulls us apart, Jed's so mad at me that he's spitting, but I don't care. My smarting face is easier to bear than the pain inside me.

I use the fight as an excuse to get out of the house and ignore Mom as she shouts at me when I take her car keys. Sherrie chases out after me and grabs my jacket.

"Get back inside, you little..." she yells, but I swing around to break her hold on me and call her every foul word I can think of. Jason follows her outside, and she snaps at him.

"Don't just stand there. Stop him!" But I slip into the car, turn the key and jam my foot hard on the accelerator. The car skids down the road. My heart is racing and I glance in the mirror. I can't tell who's driving, but they're following me down the road.

Something vile rises in my chest, something that has no name; I feel angry, hateful and yet excited at the same time. My pain is forgotten, and it feels good. How dare they try and stop me? I won't let them. I can out-drive them any day.

I fly down the road, slamming on my brakes as I turn the corner. I feel the back of the car slide beneath me, but as the steering wheel slides through my hands, the car seems to steady. Their lights blind me, so I put my foot down hard and feel the car take off.

I don't know how long we race along the roads, me storming ahead of them as they struggle to keep up. I hear a siren in the distance and my stomach does a double flip. I'm not scared, though; the siren makes me feel even more excited.

A car swerves wildly to miss me and I'm only vaguely aware that the noise I can hear in the car is me, cackling with laughter. I don't sound like me anymore, in fact I don't know who I am anymore. I'm just driven by something deep inside me to end the pain I feel, so my foot is pressed hard against the floor as the car flies down the road. I wrench the wheel this way and that as I swerve to avoid the cars coming towards me, their lights blinding me.

I holler with jubilation, ignoring the sound of horns blaring and lights flashing before me and in my rear-view mirror. I grip the steering wheel and sit forward, willing the car to go faster, and as the sound of sirens gets louder, my foot is hard on the floor. I scan my rear-view mirror again, and in that split-second the road before me changes. By the time I look back through the windshield, I see two cars baring down on me, one on the opposite side of the road, and one that's overtaking, which heads straight towards me. Although I'm driving as fast as I can there's nowhere for me to go, and with a flash of fear that feels strangely like excitement, I haul the steering wheel to the right and everything goes black...

• • • •

I pray that I'm dead, and yet there's a sinking feeling in my stomach as my senses begin to take in my surroundings. I know I can't be dead because I can hear Mom and Sherrie talking. The pain in my leg is terrible and I'm aware that I let out a moan.

"He hasn't been the same since Tom died," I hear Mom say. "I've tried to help him, but he seems to be beyond help. He seems to have a deathwish."

"You're too easy on him," Sherrie says, her voice heavy with blame. "He could have killed us."

Mom stands up for me, and as I lie still, unable to move, I'm surprised.

"I know he shouldn't have taken my car, but what did you hope to achieve by chasing him? You all could have been killed. What would I have done then?" Her voice breaks and she sobs. "Don't you know how hard this has been on me, on the boys, on Adam and Jed," and as if an afterthought, "and poor Nancy and the kids?"

Sherrie sounds angry. "What? We could have been killed tonight. We followed him to try and make him safe. What are you saying?"

I can hear Mom trying to placate Sherrie, as she always does. I can't remember a time when Mom hasn't tried to stop Sherrie from losing her temper, and as I lie here in a hospital bed with my leg stiff and raised above me, I hear Sherrie manipulate Mom.

"Don't you care about me and Jason?" She pauses while Mom struggles to find the right words. "Oh, I get it, you've always put everyone else before me, haven't you? I don't matter to you, do I?"

Mom stutters. "What, what? Don't be so stupid. I care about all of you. Why are you talking like this?"

"Oh, whatever," I hear Sherrie say, and then there's silence, except Mom calling, "Come back."

I lie still, waiting to see what's going to happen, but nothing does. Mom must have chased after Sherrie; same old story.

I can't believe that I'm not dead. It is the second time this has happened to me. How come it was so easy for Tom to die, yet it's so hard for me? Dear God, please take this away from me. I can't bear my pain, and I can't bear the guilt I feel. Please take me away.

My thoughts drift away with a sweet numbness that flows through my body, and I'm only vaguely aware that the pain in my broken leg is tempered by the same restraint that tries to smother my thoughts. I must be drugged. My hand hurts. I lift it up before me and see that I'm attached to an IV line.

When I wake up again I have no idea what day it is or what time it is. I'm thirsty and my head's swimming. I search for the call bell, and when I find it under my pillow, I press it relentlessly.

"What d'you want?" a nurse asks coldly.

"Where am I? What's happened to me?"

"What?"

"What's happened to me? My leg hurts."

"You've broken your leg, and you're lucky that you didn't kill yourself, or anyone else for that matter. There were children in those cars."

She sounds like she hates me, and I feel ashamed. I say nothing.

I lie there for what seems like hours and hours, and eventually someone comes to speak to me. He's a paramedic.

"Hey, Adam, how'ya doing? I hear that things have been a bit tough lately."

I say nothing. I don't want to talk to him. What

does he know? But he carries on talking, and despite my being irritated and sullen, hoping that he'll go away, he carries on talking.

"Y'know, I lost my best friend when I was twelve. It was the worst day of my life. Even now I don't know how I got over it. Perhaps I haven't. Grief's a weird thing. It's always there, and everyone tells you what to do, believing it to be in your best interest, but no one knows the awful pain you go through when you lose someone you love."

Although I don't want to speak to him, I listen.

"Listen, your doctor thinks that you've got problems about accepting your brother-in-law's death and he thinks it's best if you go to Beach Haven. Your mom thinks so, too."

"What? Where?"

"Beach Haven. It's a place where kids can go to sort out their feelings and work through them. It's a place that gives you back your life."

I look at him as he starts to put all my stuff into a plastic bag, and the only thought in my head is that I don't want to get my life back. Any life without Tom is a half-life. I don't know how to *be* without him in my life.

I see no point in going anywhere, yet as they sit me in a wheelchair and tell me that I'm lucky to be going to such a place, I have mixed feelings. I feel angry with my mom for agreeing to put me somewhere without talking to me about it, yet I'm glad that I'm not going home. I can't face being in the place where Tom used to be all the time. His absence is a constant reminder of the night he died and the guilt I have to live with. Our house is full of echoes of Tom—he virtually lived with us—and being there without him is awful. Although I don't know where I'm going, I'm glad that I won't have to see Kelly's face anymore, for when she cries for her dad my heart hurts so badly with pain and guilt that I want to plunge a knife into it.

Chapter Five

The paramedic straps my wheelchair into the ambulance and positions my leg in front of me. My cast stretches from my ugly big toe to my groin.

"Hey, can I be the first to write on your leg?" he asks.

I shrug. I'm glad he's having fun, but I'm not.

The ambulance jolts my wheelchair as we go over some train tracks, and I clench my teeth as pain shoots through me.

After what seems like ages, the ambulance stops and the paramedic, who hasn't stopped talking since we left the hospital, and the driver lift me out of the ambulance. I'm in front of a big building and above the entrance, painted in big letters, are the words "Beach Haven," and beneath, in smaller letters, "a place to rest and grow."

I feel apprehensive and I swallow a lot. I hate it

when the paramedic says, "Don't be scared, this is a great place."

I want to tell him that I'm not scared, but even though I feel defensive and angry because I didn't ask to come here, I say nothing. He walks through the doors beneath the sign that tells me to rest and grow, and walks down a hall.

I'm nervous and my stomach's in knots, but the paramedics shout out to people that they obviously know well.

"How're you doing? Haven't seen you for a while. Where've you been?"

A lady walks over to us and puts out her hand to shake mind.

"Hi, you must be Adam. I'm Miss Cassie, and I'll be your life-skills teacher. Hey, don't look so worried; we have a lot of fun. See you later," she adds as she walks off, waving at the ambulance men who joke with her.

They push me through a door and suddenly there are loads of people milling about, kids my age and several adults. I can feel my cheeks burning, as I seem to be forgotten while the ambulance men flirt.

A girl comes over to me and smiles.

"Hi, I'm Holly. What's your name? How'd you break your leg? Does it hurt?"

"A bit," I say, not knowing what to answer first.

"Oh, you poor thing. I broke my arm once. Oops, time to go to group."

She follows all the other kids through a door, and looks back at me. "See you later. What did you say your name was?"

"Adam," I call after her.

Suddenly it seems much quieter, and the ambulance men leave. I sit in my wheelchair with my possessions in a plastic bag by my side, and there's only one person left in the room—a woman.

She smiles at me.

"Hello, Adam, welcome to Beach Haven. I'm Miss Tina. Don't look so worried. Everyone's here to help you. All the kids you've just seen are here because they are hurting in some way. You're not alone, and while you're here we'll help you to understand your feelings and how to manage them, and even after you leave, we'll always be here for you."

I don't know what to say. I don't want to understand my feelings or manage them; I just want to be dead, like Tom.

Miss Tina pulls up a chair and sits by me.

"What you're going through right now is one of the most difficult things that anyone has to deal with," she says.

I know. Everyone keeps telling me that, but it doesn't help.

"I lost my father earlier this year and it's been terrible. It was expected; he had cancer, you see, but when it actually happened it wasn't any easier. It was still awful. I felt all kinds of things that I hadn't expected to feel, even though I thought I'd prepared myself. It was like a punch on the nose."

I grin and she smiles at me.

"I even felt angry with him. Lots of people feel anger when someone dies; it's quite normal. Most people feel anger for being left alone to cope without their loved ones, but I felt anger because he took so long to die."

I look at her, my eyebrows raised.

"I know. It sounds terrible, doesn't it? I didn't want him to die," she says quickly. "I'd just tried to prepare myself for the end but it took longer than I expected, and I wasn't prepared for that. So as each day went by and he struggled to stay alive, I didn't know what to do with myself, and I became angry at the situation. I felt so helpless. I wanted his pain to be over, and I wanted my pain to be over, too, but I was to learn that it would carry on long after he had died. And then..." she says, drawing a deep breath.

I'm listening intently.

"...And then, to make things worse, I felt guilty as well. I felt guilty because I was angry that he took so long to die. How crazy is that? But that's how it was, and I'm still dealing with it now. D'you know that doctors say that it takes at least two years to go through the grieving process."

I frown. What does that mean?

"The grieving process is an actual thing...a bit like a cold. It has a beginning, middle and end, and it makes you feel terrible while you go through it, but you *will* come through it."

She walks around the table and opens a cupboard.

"You hungry?" she says, throwing me a bag of chips as she carries on talking, and it feels as if she'd be saying these things to herself if I wasn't here sitting in a wheelchair with my rigid leg stretched before me.

"A cold rarely kills people and it's the same with grief, but it'll make you feel awful, and sometimes you wish it *would* kill you. Believe me, I know. And just the same as a cold, the symptoms may be severe or they may be mild; it's different for everyone."

She smiles at me again as she opens a bag of chips and sits back down.

"Me, I think I got the flu, my symptoms were just awful. Like I said, I felt pain, terrible pain, and awful guilt. Who was I to be angry when my poor old dad was the one dying? I was just the one watching him. Yet it was dreadful to watch him, terrible. There were moments when I'd lock myself in the bathroom and pray to God, no actually I was *begging*. I begged God to take him so that it would be over for him and for me. That's a terrible burden to bear, terrible, and part of getting through the grieving process is about forgiving yourself for the feelings you feel. D'you want a juice?"

I'm startled out of my thoughts that have just

sprung into my head out of nowhere. I nod.

She goes to a fridge and brings me an apple juice.

"Grief really *is* like having a cold. There are so many symptoms you can feel when you have a cold, and no one person experiences all the symptoms to the same degree, and everyone has a different way of dealing with them. It's the same way with grief. You may feel all kinds of feelings depending upon how close you were, or whether you felt responsible in some way, whether you felt guilt, like I felt, and then there's the awful, awful sense of loss. When you love someone and your life is full of them, their absence leaves a terrible hole in your life. You can feel incredibly empty. I understand what you're going through."

She shakes her head and stands.

"Okay, enough of this talk. I just wanted you to know that here at Beach Haven you will be surrounded by people who know how you're feeling, and who will help you in any way they can to cope with those feelings. Just be honest and understand that it's natural to feel pain when you lose someone you love. Okay! I'm going to take you to your room. I hope you like it. It faces the beach and I hope that you'll find some peace in that...I just love the beach."

She pushes my wheelchair down a hall and into a room that has green curtains and bedcovers.

"I think you should rest for awhile. The body

needs sleep to heal itself, and your leg was smashed up pretty badly."

She doesn't tell me I should be thankful to be alive, and I'm grateful for that. She helps me stand on my good leg and swing around so that I can lie on the bed. It's comfortable, and suddenly I feel very tired. She walks towards the window and opens it.

"Y'know, there's something timeless about the ocean, and it's so soothing listening to it rolling up the shore. Rest. I'll come and get you when it's dinner time, okay?"

She's gone and I allow myself to feel the softness of my bed against my tense and painful shoulders. I listen, and she's right, I can hear waves breaking outside and seagulls screeching...

I awake with a start as a man walks into my room. "Hey, Adam, how're you doing? I'm Ken. It's almost time for dinner and I know you must be hungry, I know I am."

He helps me up and I slide over into my wheelchair. It's a bit embarrassing; I feel like an old man.

"Tomorrow you can use your crutches. That'll make you feel better because you'll be more independent."

He wheels me out of my room, along a corridor and into a large room that has a sign above the door, saying, "Dining Room." He parks me at a table and calls to one of the kids who are hovering around a large table, filling their plates.

"Hey, Saul, can you fix a plate for Adam, please?

A kid with long, tight black curls turns around and nods. Holly comes over to me.

"Hey, are you all right?"

I mutter that I'm fine. Saul comes over to me and puts a plate in front of me that has fries, meat sticks and peas on it. I'm suddenly starving.

"Hi, I'm Saul."

"Adam."

"How d'you break your leg, man?"

I'm embarrassed. I don't want to tell anyone that I was driving too fast and secretly hoping that I would die like Tom.

"I was in an accident."

"Okay. Well, glad to see that you made it."

He eats his food and I dig into mine, and I'm saved from talking because my mouth's full. Holly picks at hers.

Saul walks away and moments later he returns with two plates of dessert.

"They make amazing cheesecake here."

Holly frowns at him, and gets up to get her own.

"Girls, they're so...um...moody. If I'd brought her a dessert she'd have accused me of trying to make her fat, but because I didn't bring her one, she gets all moody."

I can't help myself; I laugh and think of Sherrie.

"Yeah, they can be that way."

He laughs, too, but he stops as Holly sits back

down at the table with a large helping of cheesecake that she begins to eat defiantly.

"So why're you here?" he asks.

I clear my throat, feeling awkward.

"My doctor and my mom thought that I needed to come here."

"Why?"

I take a swig of water, and I feel embarrassed because I don't know what to say. I like Saul but he seems a bit blunt. I clear my throat again.

"They think that I'm having trouble coping with the death of my brother-in-law. That's what they think."

He looks at me.

"And what do you think?"

Holly looks at me, too, her mouth stuffed with cheesecake, and the expression on Saul's face seems to demand an answer. I'm not used to this; I'm not used to being forced to account for my thoughts or my behavior. My heart races.

"I think they're probably right," I mumble.

He nods his head, looking thoughtful and much older than he is.

"I had, or have—sorry," he says, as if to himself, "I need to own my feelings. I *have* a problem accepting the death of my father. He died a few months ago and I never got to say goodbye to him. It's been bad. I feel angry with him, yet I feel sad as well. None of this is easy, but I'm glad I'm here because I know that even though it hurts, I will work through this and come out the other side. You'll be okay, too, if you are determined to work through it."

I feel confused because I think he's cool and I want to listen to him, but at the same time I don't want to "come out the other side." I just want to make my pain go away, and right this minute I can't see how that can happen.

The next morning Ken brings me a pair of crutches, and I try to wash myself in the bathroom. I can't shower because of my leg and I feel really dirty. I hope I don't stink.

Later I hobble to the dining room for breakfast. Holly rushes over to me and pulls a chair out for me and starts fussing. I want to tell her to leave me alone, but I can't.

"I'll get you something to eat. What d'you want?"

"Whatever. I don't know."

Another girl comes over to me as I land heavily on the chair and my crutches fall to the floor.

"Hi, I'm Nancy."

I wince at her name.

"Do you want me to get you some breakfast?"

"I'm getting him some," Holly says, irritably.

"Too late," Saul says, putting a plate of eggs and sausage in front of me. The girls walk away looking angry.

"Man," Saul laughs, "they've never flocked around me like that."

Any other time I'd have been pleased, but since I ripped up Becky's pictures, I haven't been interested in girls, except...an image of the prostitute flashes into my brain and my face burns. Saul laughs louder at my embarrassment, and I'm glad he can't read my mind.

The food's good and I concentrate on it and avoid looking over at the other kids, especially Holly and Nancy, who sit at separate tables.

"What do you do here?" I ask.

"Well, it's pretty laid back. They say that it's a place to rest and grow, and that's pretty much what we do. We go to groups at least twice a day, sometimes three times, and then we're given plenty of time to think through the stuff we've worked on in group. I guess we grow in group and rest from it afterwards," he shrugs, sounding wise, and talking about things I know nothing about.

"It can be pretty scary in group to start with, but we have rules that make it feel safer. You'll get used to it. It actually feels really good. You know that everyone in the group will be there for you. You don't have to pretend anymore. You can be yourself."

I don't say anything, as the thought of being myself seems awful. I don't want to be me, nor do I want to be "honest" with a load of kids that may judge me. I already know what I did. I don't need them making me feel worse.

Saul helps me up, and I position the crutches

under my arms, trying to keep up with him as we leave the dining room and head towards a room that has a handmade sign above the door, saying "Group Room."

I sit next to Saul and suddenly I wish I hadn't eaten breakfast, as a wave of nausea flows through me. I don't know what's going to happen.

Miss Tina comes into the room and the kids go quiet.

"Today we're going to look at loss and grief. Remember, this is a safe place and we can say anything we want without fear of being judged. This is a place where we are ourselves, our true selves."

I glance around the room and another girl looks at me and smiles. A smile flickers on my face and I look away, quickly.

Miss Tina says, "I think the best way to begin to understand grief is to hear from someone who has lost someone very dear to them. Hearing about others who have lost someone they love helps us to realize that we are not alone in the grief we feel, and that it is a normal process, a normal part of life."

She gives a little cough to clear her throat and begins to read from a paper:

Your dinner's still sitting in the microwave, waiting to be heated the moment you walk through the door. I don't know how long it's been there, for time seems to have slipped into a different dimension.

It starts the moment I see a police car pull up outside, and as the words come out of the policeman's mouth, telling me that you've had a heart attack, a noise inside my head seems to drown out his words. It's the sound of my own screaming, my own denial as I back away from him, shaking my head wildly.

I tell him that he's mistaken and that I have to get the pie out of the oven before it burns. Chicken pie is your favorite dinner, I tell him, and I don't want it to be ruined. The look on his face is mingled with concern and pity, both expressions that shouldn't be on his face. I invite him in; ask him if he likes chicken pie and would he like to stay for dinner. "My husband will be home soon," I say. "Do you like sprouts?"

I walk away from him as he frowns, and stutters, "I think you should come with me."

I'm not going anywhere; it's almost time to make the gravy. I go to the oven and carefully put the steaming pie on the side to cool. The smell is exquisite. My face is flushed with pride; you've always loved my pies. The policeman reaches towards the oven and turns it off.

"No, I haven't finished yet. Don't turn it off, the dinner will be ruined," I cry.

He leads me by the arm out to his car, and everything feels wrong. I seem to have lost the ability to think properly. I can make sense of the policeman driving along the roads, and I recognize the hospital when he pulls up in front of it, but I can't make sense of why I'm there with him. I wonder whether I've fallen asleep in front of the fire and am having a bizarre dream, one that I'll wake from the moment you come through the door and hug me for making your favorite dinner.

Everyone I see at the hospital wears an expression of sympathy, and it unnerves me. I want to slap their faces. Why are they treating me this way?

And then it happens. A nurse takes my arm and guides me into a room. I feel as if my head will explode. There you are, lying there, asleep. I rush over to you and throw my arms around you, but you don't move. I shake your arm and call your name, but you lie still—gray and cold.

I can't remember getting home. Something unknown inside me has switched off my senses and rewired my thoughts.

The first thing I do is to make the gravy. The sprouts sit in their water, cold and lifeless, and the potatoes have lost their crispiness, but the pie is still magnificent. I fix your plate and set it in the microwave, waiting for you to walk through the door, and then I sit in my chair by the fire.

I'm still sitting here the next morning, and as the day slips into the night, I don't want to move. For if I can keep still, perhaps I can avoid feeling anything or think the thoughts that threaten to destroy my world.

I didn't ask them to come but your family arrives at the door and forces me to open it. They tell me to sit down and take it easy, and they seem to take over our house. They clatter about in the kitchen, throwing food away and stacking the dishwasher, and when I see them open the microwave and take out your plate, something deep down inside me bubbles up and explodes out of me.

I grab the plate from them; my heart is hammering so hard that I really think I'm going to have a heart attack myself. I'm disappointed and feel cheated when I don't. I scream at them as if they're taking you away from me.

They seem frightened by my passion, by my pain, and they let me snatch the plate back and return it to the microwave. I hear someone shouting, "Get off it, it's his favorite dinner," and I realize that it's me.

I feel a strange sense of satisfaction as I put the plate back inside the microwave; no one is going to throw away your favorite dinner, no one.

Aunt Jessie stays with me over night. I don't want her to, but she insists.

It's as if someone has invaded my body and is operating it against my will. I'm forced to wear black and go to church, and then I'm forced to watch as men dressed in black put a box with your name on it in a deep black hole. I don't feel anything really, as I know that you'll be home soon, and as your key turns in the lock I'll wake up from the worst nightmare

I've ever had and make the gravy for your favorite chicken pie. But you don't put your key in the lock, and as mold starts to form on the chicken pie in the microwave, I find it harder and harder to deny the inevitable.

I hear myself bargaining with God in desperate pleas, as I wander around the house room to room, and I swear to do anything just so the nightmare will go away and you'll walk through the door again.

My mind has slipped into a place where disjointed thoughts make perfect sense to me. If I strive to keep everything in the house the same as that awful day when the policeman said that you wouldn't be home for dinner, maybe you'll walk through the door, shake me, and wake me up.

I wander through the house—I don't know how many times—for I can't seem to sit in one place, and there on the floor is a shirt you wore to work. It's funny how dropping your clothes on the floor wherever you take them off doesn't irritate me anymore. I smile to myself and pick the shirt up, sniffing it deeply.

You're with me, I just know it. I can smell you. I smile and feel as if my heart will burst with love for you, but then a monster rears up inside me, demanding to be heard. It tells me you've gone and that I'm going crazy. A sob escapes my lips. I drop the shirt on the floor where I found it, and a small voice inside me tells me that it isn't lying in the same position I found it in, and I feel a sense of panic. I want everything to stay exactly the same as the day you stopped coming home. I nudge the shirt with my toe, trying to make it lie in exactly the same way you left it, but each time I nudge it, I can't be sure that I haven't changed its position. I run from the room, devastated and fearful.

I feel sick constantly and can't eat. I don't want to eat, for eating keeps a person alive and I don't want to be alive without you. The thought of putting anything in my mouth to satisfy me is repugnant and I don't think I'll ever eat again.

I'm startled by banging on the door, and I only open it because whoever's there refuses to leave. I don't really hear what they're saying; something about being there if I need them. What're they talking about? I don't need anyone other than you. I get rid of them quickly, as I long to be alone in our house, with everything about you still vibrant and alive. Yet their faces feed the monster within me, the one that rears its head to tell me that I'm kidding myself that you'll be home soon, and this is all a misunderstanding.

I slam the door loudly, and the sound stays in my head as a reminder of my defiance. I don't want anyone's help because I don't need it. There's been a terrible mistake. You'll be home in a minute, and I'll have your dinner on the table; it's in the microwave, waiting.

I find myself pacing, without a destination. I can't even begin to imagine being in our home without you in it. I chase the thoughts away, thoughts that belong to the monster inside me who is determined to be heard. I feel as if I'm a spectator, looking down on someone I barely know, and as the monster begins to rear up again, I hear myself mumbling desperately. "I'll do anything, provided that you'll come home. I'll go to church every Sunday. I'll give to the poor, and I'll even take in orphaned children. Please, just tell me that you're going to come home any minute."

The silence—as my prayers are left unanswered—is broken by a noise that surrounds me. The monster finally breaks free and consumes me with the truth. I'm forced to listen, there's no escaping it. You are dead, and I'm never going to see you again. I begin to cry and I don't know how long it goes on. Time has no meaning for me anymore as I sob. It consumes me and I long for death to take me away from the pain that ravages through my body and soul, yet nothing saves me from the agony of losing you.

My knees are rocking against the hard floor and my fists are clenched. I'm moaning. Deep within me I recognize that I've lost it, but I don't care. The thought of living my life without you is too awful, and so I howl and rock; the pain in my knees reminds me that I'm alive when you aren't.

Miss Tina puts the papers down and looks at us. It's so quiet in the room that you can hear a pin drop.

Chapter Six

"What d'you think?" Miss Tina asks us, her voice breaking the silence in the room.

"She sounds crazy to me," a kid says, and others agree with him.

"Which bit sounds crazy?" she asks.

Nancy says, "Keeping his dinner in the microwave even though she must have realized that her husband was dead; after all, she saw his body and went to his funeral."

Miss Tina nods her head. "Yes, I guess that does sound a little crazy, but grief can make you do things like that and they seem perfectly reasonable to you at the time."

I glance around the room and some kids are frowning.

"Do I seem sane to you?" she asks, and all the kids say, "Yes."

"Well, when my grandson died as a baby, the grief I felt was so bad that my thinking was changed. It really did feel as if time had stood still, as if everything was in slow motion, and as if the world had slipped off its axis. I thought things that would seem crazy to anyone who wasn't grieving."

"Like what?" Saul asks.

Something flashes across her face—something painful; it's a look I've seen each time I look in the mirror.

"I couldn't bear to think of my beautiful grandson lying in a box in the ground and being cold for all eternity, so I crocheted a beautiful white gown to keep him warm, and my friend knitted him a pair of lacy socks to keep his feet warm. There's nothing worse than cold feet."

Everyone's quiet, and suddenly I understand what she's saying, as an image of Tom's grave and the rose I threw in, which floated in the rainwater, flash into my mind. I remember that I'd thought he'd be wet for all eternity, and the thought had been perfectly reasonable to me at the time.

"It gave me comfort," Miss Tina says. "Part of my brain told me that he was dead and couldn't feel anything, but another part that was attached to my emotions needed soothing, and making him warm clothes was what I needed to do to soothe that part of myself."

Nancy speaks out. "So in the paper you read, did

the lady find comfort in keeping her husband's dinner in the microwave?"

"Yes, I think she did. The paper shows that when a human being is faced with trauma, their thinking is altered. The human mind is expert at reducing tensions or pain so that a person can cope. The lady was in such pain that she wanted to die, but her mind employed strategies to soothe her. These strategies are called 'defense mechanisms,' and they defend against the person feeling intolerable psychological pain. Keeping the chicken pie in the microwave was her way of hanging on to the belief that her husband was going to come home, and that helped her to cope in the first few days after her husband died. Like I said, the human brain is incredible, it can allow a person to operate as if on 'automatic pilot,' and yet think about something else entirely. It seems that when a person goes through something traumatic, the brain 'splits'; a part of the brain enables the body to function normally but the thinking part seems to disappear somewhere. Have any of you ever felt that you've missed time? When my grandson died there were great chunks of time that I couldn't account for. I couldn't remember driving home. It used to frighten me."

I shiver. I know what she's talking about because I couldn't remember having driven down town. My mind was a complete blank.

"Part of my brain enabled me to do the things I

needed to do without thinking about, but then I'd 'disappear' somewhere inside my head; it's called 'disassociation,' and it happens when you suffer shock. I remember being locked in a place where I could barely breathe because I was in such pain."

She falters for a moment and the room is totally silent.

"God forgive me, but I didn't want to live. The pain was so awful that I just wanted it to go away. Then I felt guilty. I was trapped in a place where my thinking was totally focused upon my grandson. I became locked in a battle with God, begging him to turn back time so that none of it would have happened. It was only later that I realized how distorted my thoughts were. It was frightening, and I felt totally alone."

I swallow hard as she stands up, walks to a flip-chart and writes.

"Dr. Kubler-Ross, a famous doctor who studied grief, stated that the grieving process has five stages. She writes in big letters: DENIAL, ANGER, BARGAINING, DEPRESSION, ACCEPTANCE. People don't always go through these stages in this order, and they may get stuck at any stage. Sometimes it can take a very long time to get to the acceptance stage."

She sits back down.

"Let's go through the paper and see if we can pick out these five stages in this poor lady's grief."

She hands us all a copy of the paper, and as we

read she sits there waiting for us to shout out our comments.

Saul's the first to speak. "She says that time seemed to have slipped into a different dimension. Is that denial?"

"I think it is. Remember how the brain seems to be able to split so that the body is able to complete tasks automatically. Think about it, if your brain is not paying attention to the tasks it's doing, then the nature of time will be misunderstood. Imagine finding yourself somewhere else and not remembering how you got there; your ability to discern how much time has passed will be impaired."

I know just what she means because I had no idea about time when I drove away from the house when all I could think about was Tom.

"She didn't seem to hear what the policeman said," a girl says. "Is that denial, too?"

"Yes, Chelsea. Look at what she did. She focused upon making the dinner, in order to avoid having to accept what the policeman was saying," Miss Tina says.

A guy speaks out. "Yeah, but don't you think it was weird that she asked him to stay for dinner?"

I look around trying to gauge the kids' reaction.

"Yes, I agree, it does sound weird, doesn't it?" Miss Tina says. "But when you think about it and try to understand what's going on in the brain of someone who's suffering from grief, it makes sense. The lady was desperate to keep things normal. Asking the policeman to stay for dinner was her attempt to normalize things, and she did this to reduce the shock and the psychological pain she was feeling. She was in the process of denial. Her behavior was normal for anyone beginning the grief process."

Nancy speaks out. "So, what was going through her head when everyone at the hospital was being sympathetic? Surely she would have accepted it then."

"I think she was fighting against the inevitable, don't you? She knew something was wrong. The truth was filtering into her brain and when she saw the body she couldn't deny it anymore."

Saul says, "So how come she still kept his dinner in the microwave? I mean, she did it even after she'd been to his funeral. She had to have accepted that he was dead then, surely?"

Miss Tina leans forward. "Try and remember what happens to a human being when they're traumatized. Her brain was battling to find a way to reduce her pain, and if she could believe that it was all a nightmare, one that she'd awaken from, then she could prevent herself from feeling the full force of the pain. Did you notice that she became angry, especially when her in-laws came around to 'help'?"

"Oh," Chelsea says loudly, as if she's just had a brainwave. "Oh, maybe her anger was really fear. She was scared that they would force her to accept that her husband was dead, and she couldn't cope with that, so she became angry in order to stop them."

Miss Tina smiles at her.

"Well done, Chelsea. That's exactly right. The part of her brain that was desperate to avoid facing the truth reacted with anger and aggression. She scared them into leaving the dinner in the microwave, and for a short time she could kid herself that everything would be all right. But it was only for a short time. The presence of Aunt Jessie was a silent reminder that something was wrong, and it would have filtered into the part of her brain that had separated, that was disassociated. Denial can only last a certain amount of time before the 'evidence' becomes overwhelming and the brain shifts back towards being able to accept reality."

Miss Tina stands up. "Let's have a break. Come back in thirty minutes."

I follow the kids out of the room. Some head towards the dining room, others towards the living room, a big room with squashy sofas that I know I'll never get out of if I dare to sit in them. I lurch after them on my crutches and follow Saul, who goes through a door that leads to a playground outside. I struggle with the door.

A guy my age comes up behind me.

"Hey, let me help you."

I feel stupid but grateful, and hobble through the

doorway while he holds it open.

"I'm R.J. How'd you break your leg?" he says, walking slowly towards the other kids who are hanging out around the swings on the playground.

"I was driving too fast, I guess," I say, hoping that he won't ask me any more questions.

"Hey Adam," Saul says. "How're you doin'? What d'you think of group?" He's laughing but I don't feel that he's being mean.

"Heavy," I say. I sit on a wooden bench as some other kids hang around.

"Yeah, it is. It's good though. It makes you think things that you'd never think of on your own. It's helped me so much. Y'know, sometimes I don't even feel as if I'm the same person I was when I first came here."

"How long have you been here?"

"Two months. I know, it's a long time, but I was a mess when I first got here. I was lucky; if I hadn't been brought here I'd have died, I know I would. I couldn't stand the pain and all I wanted to do was kill myself to make it go away. Hey, Chelsea, how're you doin'?"

I swing around to follow his eyes and Chelsea walks past with Nancy, who looks at me and smiles. I look away.

"She's amazing," Saul says. "When she first got here she was crazy, and I mean *crazy*. I understand everything Miss Tina said in group about part of your brain doing its own thing, even though you're able to function physically, because when Chelsea first came here she was wired. I mean, when she first came here she was nuts."

Looking at Chelsea now, I can't imagine that she could ever have been "nuts."

"She'd been babysitting her little sister when a fire broke out. It wasn't anyone's fault. It was something wrong with the electrical system, and when she woke up in the middle of the night the house was filled with smoke. She tried to get her sister out, but it was impossible."

I shake my head, imagining how I'd feel if little Kelly were stuck in the house and I couldn't rescue her. I shiver, even though I can feel the warmth of the sun on my shoulders.

"She screamed a lot in her sleep when she first got here. It took her ages to stop blaming herself. She went through all the first stages of the grieving process and, d'you know, watching her and helping her through it has helped me to understand the grief process. If I had just read about it, I don't think it would have made much sense to me, but watching Chelsea has brought it alive for me."

I shield my eyes and look at him as R.J. comes back with a can of soda for each of us. I take a deep swig from the can and we fall silent. Chelsea comes over to us and sits on the bench next to me.

"What're you talking about?" she asks.

"I was telling Adam how amazing you are," Saul tells her.

"Quit, will you?" She grins, punches him on the arm and then looks at me.

"Well, Adam, what d'you think of Beach Haven?"

"I didn't know what to expect. It's a bit freaky being among people who are so honest."

"Yeah, I know. It took me ages to get used to it, but once I realized that everyone here is honest about their feelings and wants to work through them, it's amazing how safe you feel. I've never felt this safe before in my whole life."

She smiles at me and says, "You'll get used to it and you'll feel safe, too; everyone here does."

I feel strange. I don't know what I feel. I don't know if I want to feel safe like Chelsea describes, because I just want my pain and the awful emptiness that's inside me to go away. I'm not sure I even understand what she means by feeling "safe." I don't answer her, and I sip my soda slowly so that I don't have to talk.

The sun beats down on my face and my thoughts drift, slowly drowning out the sounds of the kids laughing and the seagulls screeching above us. There's a man on the shore who throws a fishing line out into the surf, and as he holds his line high with one hand, he scrabbles about with the other to position a stool in the right place in the sand. He sits, and a black dog sits beside him until the man throws a stick and it darts after it. My thoughts drift away to a riverbank where Tom and I had gone fishing. He'd shown me how to cast the line, and it had taken me ages to get it right but he had been patient. We had sat for hours on the same type of collapsible stools, our asses numb, waiting for a fish to bite...

"Hey, Adam, c'mon, the bell's rung. We have to go in."

My can of soda is empty but I can't remember drinking it. Saul helps me to my feet and I put my crutches under my armpits awkwardly and hobble after them towards the door. I had been miles away; I'd lost the ability to hear the sounds around me even though, now, I can hear the kids calling out to each other and the seagulls' screeching is relentless. I can't remember drinking my soda. My thoughts are racing as I follow the other kids. Has my brain just "split" in the same way that Miss Tina was talking about? My body remained sitting upright and lifted my can of soda to my mouth, yet I have no recollection of doing it. All I can remember is being locked in a place where there was only Tom and me, fishing, like the man on the beach. I think I understand what Miss Tina was talking about.

I follow the other kids inside and drag myself towards the Group Room. My armpits hurt.

Miss Tina is sitting in her chair, smiling, waiting for us to settle down.

"What d'you make of the phrase, 'Something unknown inside me had switched off my senses and rewired my thoughts'? That's what the lady wrote in the paper. What does she mean?" she asks, when we get quiet. She looks at me and says, "Adam?"

I can feel myself blushing, but Chelsea catches my eye and nods at me.

I fight the feeling of fear that leaps upon me, and I ask her to repeat the phrase. The time she takes gives me a moment to try and battle my fear and to think. I think about what's just happened to me outside on the playground. I don't know if I make any sense but I speak anyway.

"When she says, 'something unknown,' she could mean that she was not used to feeling that way, and 'switching off her senses' could be about...what was it you called it?"

"Disassociation, feeling separate and distant from reality," Miss Tina prompts.

"And 'rewired my thoughts' could be about her brain not working properly and about her denying the truth," I say, my face burning.

"Well done," Miss Tina says, as my eyes shoot to the floor and then glance around the room, taking in Holly, Nancy and Chelsea who are all smiling at me.

Saul nudges me in the ribs and I wince. "Smart ass," he whispers, grinning at me. I suddenly feel less anxious.

Miss Tina continues. "Absolutely. When we're first faced with grief it *is* 'something unknown,' and it's frightening. Remember, the body's response to trauma is to disassociate...Chelsea, what does that word mean?"

"It means to feel separate from reality," she says with ease.

"That's right. So, Adam, once she'd experienced the trauma and her brain had 'disassociated,' she had to deal with the thoughts that were trying to break through. There's never a time when the brain isn't thinking, and even though she didn't want to think about her husband's death, her brain was working overtime and thinking anyway."

I'm anxious because if she's going to ask me another question, I don't think I can answer it; this is getting deep.

"So...her brain was trying to connect the part that was in denial about her husband's death to the part that was trying to make sense of everything. She still wasn't ready to accept the truth, so she settled for a warped way of looking at things. Her thoughts were 'rewired'; she was in denial."

She looks at us, and the silence in the room is deafening.

"The human body is destined to be emotionally healthy, to be sane, and so even though she longed to be engulfed in denial so that she didn't have to endure the awful pain she felt, her brain kept trying to force her to face it."

She stands up and walks to the flipchart, pointing to the words "anger," and "bargaining."

"Give me an example of when the lady experienced these two parts of the grieving process," she says.

Saul says, "She was angry when his family tried to take over."

"Yes, she was. A person going through the grieving process can feel angry for all sorts of reasons. The most common is, 'How could you leave me?' Often a bereaved person can feel anger towards God, or towards anyone involved in the death."

"I felt angry with my dad for not telling me that my mom was dying," a kid says. "He didn't allow me time to say goodbye. I just thought that she'd get better and so I never got to say the things I really wanted to say to her."

"Yeah," Chelsea says, "but perhaps he was trying to protect you in some way."

"Yeah, perhaps he didn't know how to handle it himself. You shouldn't be so hard on him; he was grieving, too," R.J. says.

"I know that now," the kid says, "but I didn't at the time and it was hard. I was really angry with him; I felt he shut me out."

"Perhaps he was trying to protect you from the pain *he* was feeling," Nancy says.

The kid goes very red in the face and looks as if he's going to cry. "I know, but I just wish he'd talked to me and let me know what was happening. It was bad enough to lose my mom, but it made it harder by not being able to say goodbye."

He falls silent and I'm left with my own regrets about Tom and all the things I never had the chance to tell him.

"Can you see that it's easier to place the anger you feel on to someone other than the person who has died, or on to yourself for the regret you may feel?" Miss Tina says, breaking into our thoughts. "Very often we get hooked into a game of, 'what if?' when we lose someone we love. Have any of you ever thought, 'What if I'd done something differently?'"

I don't know what makes my hand rise above me.

"Adam?" Miss Tina asks gently.

Something seems to settle over me, and it strips away everything that's held me together. I swallow hard and then, to my shame and embarrassment, my eyes prickle with hot burning tears. I'm morti-fied and I want to run from the room, but I can't; my crutches are laid lifelessly on the floor in front of me. Something seems to happen inside me that I can't stop. I feel broken in two, and as my breaths come in ragged gasps, I know that the sobbing echo-ing around the room is coming from me, from my broken heart.

I don't know how much time has past before Miss Tina gently says, "Adam, what is it that you believe you could have done differently?"

I know everyone's looking at me, and although I want to run away, I can't, but neither can I sit here and say nothing. The words seem as if they're coming from someone else.

"My brother-in-law wouldn't be dead if it weren't for me..."

I'm only vaguely aware that I'm speaking out in front of all these kids that I don't know, but nothing seems to stop me until I've finished. My head is in my hands and I feel numb, as if I've disappeared somewhere, chased by guilt snapping at my heels, like an angry dog.

No one comes to my rescue and a flashing thought reminds me what the kids told me: In this place, people don't rescue each other; everyone has to deal with their own pain. There's a part of me that sits far above, watching. Saul has a box of tissues in his hand and he holds them out. When I realize that no one is going to put their arm around me and whisper that it's all going to be okay, I take a tissue from Saul and blow my nose noisily.

"Adam, did you murder your brother-in-law?" Miss Tina says, sharply.

"No!" I state angrily. How dare she suggest such a thing? I'm jolted back into the room where everyone's staring at me.

"Then how is it your fault he's dead?" she asks pointedly.

I don't know how to answer without damning myself. I was selfish that night. I needed a ride so that I could pick up Becky at the right time in order to make her birthday party a surprise.

"How is it your fault that Tom's dead?" Miss Tina persists.

I sit in silence for what seems an endless amount of time, and after I draw a deep intake of breath, my voice seems to get louder. I wipe my tears away on my sleeve. I tell them about the night that Kelly hurt herself and how my mind had been focused only upon Becky's birthday.

There's snot pouring down onto my lip but I'm beyond caring as I blurt everything out amidst sobs. I don't care if anyone thinks I'm a baby; I don't care about anything anymore. I can't bear the pain of keeping it all inside me.

I don't even sound like me anymore. "If it wasn't for Becky's birthday party none of this would have happened. I hate her..."

I feel as if I've vomited on the floor. Everything inside me has landed in the middle of the room, and as I catch my breath, I'm aware that the room is silent.

I wipe the endless trail of snot on my sleeve and try to steady my breathing. I feel dizzy and sick, and then fearful. What will all these kids think of me now that they can see the real me, and what I've done? It's all my fault and there's nowhere for me to hide anymore.

No one says anything and the silence in the room becomes intolerable. My breathing gradually calms, and I gain control of my nose by sniffing and swallowing deeply.

Saul is the first to speak, and despite my pain, I feel surprised; I thought it would be Miss Tina.

"Hey, man, it's not your fault Tom died, but it's not your girlfriend's fault either."

I have a sudden urge to punch him, but other kids speak out and they all say the same.

I glance around the room, not wanting to accept what they're saying, so I look towards Miss Tina. The kids go quiet.

"It's normal to search for answers after an awful tragedy," she says. "Everyone does it. They ask themselves, 'What could I have done differently?' And it's normal to beat yourself up over it. It almost gives you a reason that you can understand for the awful pain you feel. But, you know, unless you have committed murder, and in that case it *would* be your fault that someone is dead, no matter what you did or didn't do, it is *not* your fault that someone else died. Everyone has a choice as to how they behave and what decisions they make."

I know that my face is contorted with pain and disbelief. I don't want to listen to the things she's saying because I know that I deserve my pain. A stray thought flashes through my mind. *I don't want to listen to the things she's saying because I need my pain.*

My head starts to spin as the thought settles into

my consciousness. This is crazy, I don't *need* pain. I'd give anything to make the pain stop. I don't know what to say or do. Suddenly I feel more tired than I've ever felt in my life and I just want it all to end. I know it's against my beliefs, but at this moment I want to kill myself. I hate myself all over again as I burst into a new set of tears that seem to have more energy than the last bunch.

This time Saul puts his hand on my shoulder and I'm too tired to shrug him off. There's a tiny, insignificant voice deep within me that tells me to grab his hand, as I'm about to lose my sanity and he can help me to hold onto it. The thought doesn't feel as if it comes from me but from someone else who's inhabiting my body. But even as I think it, somewhere deep inside me the word "disassociation" registers with me, and the thought tries to force me to stay focused, to stay in the room where my broken body sits nursing my broken heart. And that thought stays with me, holding me back from the edge of a deep, dark precipice that has my name on it, one that makes goose-bumps shiver all over my body.

Chapter Seven

My head's spinning, and I feel sick. I feel as if the core of me is shriveled with pain; I hurt so much. It's more than I can bear, and I feel as if I'm about to pass out. I can't think straight and my thoughts seem to be floating away somewhere. I want it all to go away. I'm surprised when Miss Tina's voice breaks through the confusion raging inside me.

"What do you mean when you say that you want it all to go away? Do you feel suicidal?"

I didn't realize that I'd spoken out loud. I nod and damn myself for starting to cry all over again. My ears feel blocked by my own sobbing and sniffing, and I can barely feel my body.

Miss Tina raises her voice slightly though not in anger.

"Adam, I know you feel terrible and it's natural to want it all to go away. No one wants to feel so much pain, but I want to ask you a question. Can you hear me?"

I look at her although my eyes are swimming with tears, and her question seems to grab hold of me. Why shouldn't I be able to hear her? She's only a few feet away from me, but the fact that she asks me if I can hear her tells me that she knows I'm not really inside my head. She knows that I've floated away somewhere.

"Can you hear me?" she asks again, and I nod. "Ask yourself what Tom would think and feel if you were to commit suicide because you can't stand the pain of losing him."

Her words cut through me like a knife and jolt my senses back into the room again. My tears stop instantly, and I sniff the snot running out of my nose into the back of my throat. I feel angry with her for forcing me to think as if I were Tom. It hurts.

My eyes are still wet, and I wipe them on the back of my hand. My head's spinning as I glance around the room, and all the kids are looking at me waiting for an answer.

Miss Tina looks at me and doesn't look away.

"Adam, what would Tom feel, if you were to commit suicide?"

The pain inside me makes me want to run from the room and get away from everyone's prying eyes, but my broken leg won't allow me to escape their insistence that I answer. I feel angry. This is my pain.

I don't have to answer anyone, but as I feel trapped in my seat by my leg and their silence, I'm forced to answer.

I try to shut them out by hanging my head in my hands, and mumbling into my lap.

"He'd be devastated."

"I'm sorry, Adam," Miss Tina says in an overly loud voice, "I didn't quite hear you. What would Tom feel if you committed suicide because you couldn't stand the pain of losing him?"

I look up at all of them staring at me, and I feel a flash of hatred towards them for making me face this.

"I said, he'd feel devastated!" I shout, not caring anymore.

No one says anything, and suddenly I'm embarrassed. I lower my voice. "He'd be devastated," I whisper, as the words hit me.

We sit and stare at each other. As the words and their meaning sink in, I know that no matter how terrible the pain gets, I can never kill myself. I don't know where Tom is, or if there's a heaven—I pray there is—but if there is and Tom is watching and feels as much love for me as I feel for him, then I *know* with absolute certainty that he *would* be devastated if I were to kill myself.

Although I feel trapped by my own realization that I can't get away from the pain I feel, I also feel a bit safer than I felt a minute ago. I don't know what's happening to me...it's all too hard.

Miss Tina speaks and breaks the silence in the room.

"Suicide is *never* the answer, no matter how much pain you feel. The grieving process *is* painful; it's probably the most painful thing you'll ever have to deal with..."

I wince with irritation as I hear that sentence for the hundredth time.

"...But suicide is not the answer. The way you feel now will lessen in time. I know you may not believe me because it feels so bad right now that you can't imagine life can ever get any better, but it will. Try and see the grieving process as a journey, one that is hard and painful, but one where the destination is never in doubt. You will make it and you will get there, safe and sound. You will get through this and find yourself in a place where you can smile at your memories of the one you've lost, for you haven't really lost them. Those we love live in our hearts and in our memories, and we can feel the love we shared just by thinking about them."

I don't know what to think for my thoughts seem fragmented, lost, as if they're a puzzle thrown into the wind, its pieces scattered and meaningless. I hear Miss Tina's words, and although I feel skeptical, there's something soothing about what she's saying. I'm confused and my head continues to spin.

Chelsea breaks the silence.

"I tried to kill myself after my little sister was burned. I couldn't bear it. I'd visit her in the hospital and when they tried to change her dressings, she'd scream in agony. I just couldn't handle it. I felt so guilty that I just wanted my own pain to go away, and so I tried to kill myself."

She starts to cry quietly and no one rushes to comfort her. I sit up in my seat a little to watch her being real with herself, and with us. After a while she looks up and takes a deep breath.

"I feel so bad about it now. I hurt my parents badly. They almost lost my sister and then nearly lost me, too. I didn't realize that I was being selfish at the time; I just wanted the pain to go away."

Miss Tina smiles at her, and says, "It would have been a tragedy to have lost you, Chelsea. No one's meant to lose their life in such a way. Life is a precious gift, even though it can be hard and painful at times."

Chelsea smiles at her.

The phone rings and Miss Tina jumps up to get it.

"Yes, in about ten minutes," she says.

She sits back down.

"So, let's go over what we've looked at today. We've looked at the grieving process and seen that there are five stages. We've looked at denial, anger and bargaining. When a person begins to bargain with God or a higher power, something begins to happen in the brain. It's as if the truth is beginning to seep in; it's like the last attempt to remain in denial. 'I'll do anything if you'll just make this go away' is the plea on a bereaved person's lips. But, you know, the process of bargaining is the very beginning of the healing process, and as the truth seeps into the brain, the grieving process starts to take another direction."

I'm trying to make sense of what she's saying, but it's hard because my head is still spinning really badly and I feel sick.

"So what happens when the bargaining fails to work and the person you've lost won't and can't come back? The brain is forced to accept the inevitable, and for most people the truth hits them like a runaway freight train; there's no escape, and that's when depression hits them. It can be the worst part of the grieving process because when you're depressed, it's like being in a deep, dark pit that you can't drag yourself out of. Who can tell me what the symptoms of depression are?"

The kids start calling out.

"Crying."

"Not eating."

"Eating to fill the emptiness."

"Drinking alcohol."

"Sleeping all the time."

"Not caring about washing or wearing clean clothes."

"Taking drugs."

"Staying away from everyone."

"Not caring about anything."

"Doing things that are dangerous because you don't care about what happens to you."

Miss Tina smiles and she looks pleased.

"Yes, all these are symptoms of depression. Y'know, depression can be pretty bad, in fact it's awful, but it *is* a normal part of the grieving process and it *will* pass."

Suddenly something happens inside my head; a thought lands heavily like a jumbo jet. No one has ever told me that I've been suffering from depression, but suddenly it becomes clear to me. I'm not going crazy after all, I'm just going through the grieving process and I've gotten stuck at the depression stage. The kids' answers stay in my head, and I realize that I'm not alone.

Miss Tina's face suddenly brightens. She glances at her watch and strains to look out of the window.

"Okay, let's bring this session to an end. The worst part of the grieving process is denial, although most people would probably say that the depression stage is the worst, but denial keeps you 'stuck.' There's no recovery if you get stuck in the denial stage. But if you can understand what happens to the brain in a person who has lost someone, or in those people who have suffered trauma, you can understand and make sense of it. Making sense of your thought processes and your feelings will set you free, because not understanding them will make you feel as if you're going crazy."

I know just what she means.

"We have learned about 'disassociation,' which means...?" She grins at us.

"It means to feel separate from reality," Chelsea says again.

"But remember, there's never a time when the brain isn't thinking, and although the natural response to severe pain is to 'disassociate,' in order to protect yourself against extreme psychological pain, the brain finds a way to force you to face the truth. And once the truth filters through, there's nowhere to go but to accept the truth. That's when you hit the depression stage."

I know she's telling me the truth because everything she's saying describes how it's been for me since Tom died.

"But, the good news is that once you've hit this stage, even though it feels worse than anything you have ever felt before, you're almost there. You've almost made it through the journey of the grieving process."

I feel a sudden surge of hope.

Miss Tina glances at her watch again, stands, and looks out of the window. She smiles, walks towards the double doors, and opens them.

Suddenly I'm drawn towards the sound of seagulls screeching outside. I limp behind the kids, who follow Miss Tina with ease outside onto the playground, as I try to ignore the pain in my armpits where my crutches are digging into me.

"Cool," some of the girls cry.

Ken is sitting on a bench with at least twenty colorful balloons bobbing just above his head, all tied to his wrists. They're the sort you buy at the fair, like the one I bought for Becky's birthday. I swallow hard.

Ken grins and tells us to grab his feet if he starts to drift away. He looks silly and I laugh along with the others.

Miss Tina sits next to him as we find somewhere to sit, and she doesn't start talking until I've settled myself on a swing and my crutches are lying on the ground.

"These balloons represent the human brain. Each one of them is a part of the brain and you'll know from your science classes at school that different parts of the brain have different functions. One part deals with balance, another with automatic movement, and other parts deal with your senses. A massive part of the brain deals with thoughts and memories.

"See how all these balloons are roughly the same distance above Ken's head, well, these balloons and their position represent the human brain when it's functioning as it should, during times where the person doesn't experience any great trauma. All these parts of the brain are available to use as much as each other. Some of these balloons represent the parts of the human brain that operate on 'automatic pilot.' They work so that we can drive the car to work, to walk along the street, run when it starts to rain, and to eat, drink and go to the bathroom without thinking about it."

The balloons bob about, bumping into each other as if they're jostling for position.

"For most of the time all these balloons coexist together; they bob about next to each other as one, and here's Ken, comfortable that his brain is doing what it's supposed to be doing."

We look at Ken who is grinning at us, and as he moves his arms, the balloons bump noiselessly into each other just above his head.

"Something different happens when a person experiences trauma. When something happens that makes a person 'wobble' emotionally, things change."

"What d'you mean by 'wobble emotionally'?" Nancy asks.

"Most of the time people feel emotionally stable; they know who they are and what's expected of them. They expect those closest around them to remain the same, to always be there and to behave in a certain way. When any one of those things changes, it can cause a deep sense of anxiety, especially if something traumatic has happened to you."

The seagulls are screeching above us and Miss Tina raises her voice to be heard.

"What kinds of things?" a girl asks.

"The death of someone close to you, being raped, when your parent leaves you, when your parent doesn't want you anymore, injury, when you split up with the partner you love with all your heart...there are so many things that can cause trauma," Miss Tina says. "So when a person experiences trauma, when they're in shock, something happens to the brain. Watch!"

The balloons continue to bob roughly at the same height above Ken's head, but when Miss Tina nods at him, he fiddles with some of the strings that are wrapped around his wrists and most of the balloons rise far above his head. I look up, shielding my eyes from the glaring sun. There are just a few balloons that stay immediately above his head but the rest are bobbing wildly, high above him.

I think I get it.

"What you see now represents 'denial' and 'dis-association.' These balloons," Miss Tina points to the few balloons that are just above Ken's head, "are where they're supposed to be. These parts of the brain represent the parts that enable Ken to carry on with his life, to operate on 'automatic pilot,' so that he can 'function,' and he hopes that people around him will think he's all right, and will leave him alone. But the parts of the brain that help him

to think clearly and work stuff out are up there."
She looks above us to the mass of brightly colored,
bobbing balloons.

"Ken's shock and denial are so great that he cannot think straight; his 'thoughts are rewired,' like
the lady in the paper we read. These parts of the
brain that have 'disassociated' are still part of the
brain and they still work, but in the process of denial, these parts of the brain have drifted away to
a place temporarily out of reach. They're still there
but it's as if they're in hiding. The brain does this in
an attempt to protect the person from experiencing
terrible pain or shock."

The wind nips at the balloons and they move
constantly, letting us know that they are still there.
Several seagulls swoop towards the balloons high
above Ken's head and the kids laugh. Ken pulls a face
and shakes his fists at them, causing all the balloons
to go crazy. He looks like a wild man—and he looks
pretty funny. I laugh, too, as he shouts, "Hey, get off
my brain." It seems to take ages for his "brain" to
stop bouncing about.

Miss Tina giggles and after a while, when we all
quiet down, she starts to speak again.

"Who can tell me what the final part of the grieving process is?"

Saul calls out, "Acceptance."

"Yes, acceptance," Miss Tina says, her voice
solemn and quiet, so quiet that I strain to hear as

the waves crash upon the shore just feet away from the playground. "Acceptance is the last stage of the grieving process and it allows you to move forward, to go on with your life without feeling guilty about anything, without feeling guilty that you are alive and the other person isn't."

My head starts to spin again.

"That doesn't mean that you won't still feel the awful pain of missing someone you love dearly—absolutely not. The pain may last long after you've accepted that your loved one has died. Acceptance means that you are able to accept the facts about your loved one's death and are able to live with it, so that you can carry on living your own life. How do you know when you've reached this final stage?"

She looks around at all of us as no one raises their hand.

"The answer is, you know that you've reached the acceptance stage of the grieving process when you're able to use all of your brain again. When you are able to accept all the facts about your loved one's death, and when you're able to think about your memories without falling to pieces. I think that's the whole point about grieving," she says wistfully, as if she's disappeared somewhere and is talking to herself. "I think it's about coming to terms with the fact that, although you can no longer be next to the person you love physically, that person is always with you in your heart and in your memories. If you can reach that point, you can see the loss differently, and once you realize that the person still lives in your heart and memories, then they haven't really gone. They still exist. That's acceptance."

She seems to shake herself and then looks at Ken. He starts to wind some of the strings around his wrists, and one by one the balloons are pulled back towards the others that continue to bob just above his head, his "automatic pilot" balloons.

Miss Tina smiles at us and says, "Gradually as you accept that the person you love has died, you begin to regain the use of the parts of your brain that seemed to have 'disappeared' when you were in denial. You can think clearly, work things out and be objective. You will be able to recognize that nothing you did caused the death, unless of course you murdered someone, and that blame is a useless waste of energy."

Miss Tina raises her voice slightly as the seagulls continue to shriek overhead. "So, we've learned about the grief process. These balloons represent what happens when we're in denial, and denial can be present throughout the first four stages of the grieving process. It is only when we reach the acceptance stage that we beat denial."

The balloons are all bobbing now at roughly the same height above Ken's head, and he looks sheepish.

"I've got my brain back," he says, and we laugh. He stands up. "Here, you can all have a bit of my brain if you want."

Everyone gets a balloon except me; I don't want one. Balloons remind me of Becky's birthday and the night Tom died.

Miss Tina says, "That's enough for today. See you all tomorrow. Have fun tonight."

"What's happening tonight?" I ask Saul.

"Oh, you'll see."

Chelsea hangs back with us as the rest of the kids go inside.

"What're you going to make tonight?" she asks Saul.

I look at both of them as if I'm a spectator at a game of tennis.

"What's happening tonight?" I ask again.

Chelsea grins. "Once a week we make something that represents what we're feeling or how we see ourselves, and each week we use a different material. It's fun. Last week we used food and I made a big meringue."

I frown at her.

"It represented my tough exterior but my soft inside..." She suddenly looks coy and grins. "...And my sweetness."

Saul laughs. "I made chocolate pudding to describe myself. I'm dark, satisfying, comforting and sweet, but too much of me will make you sick."

I laugh and Chelsea punches him playfully on the arm. I briefly wonder what I would have made.

Chelsea says, "I heard Miss Cassie say that tonight we're going to use clay. I can't wait. My uncle has a pottery shop and he lets me make little pots on the wheel. It's messy but fun."

She walks off towards the door and Saul and I follow her.

At dinner everyone is bragging about what they're going to make. I feel anxious. I've never made anything before, except a mess.

I follow the kids into a classroom that looks messy. There are deep sinks, pottery wheels, easels, pots of paint and a slab of clay dumped on every table. I stand there not knowing where to sit...I don't want to take anyone's place as the kids all seem to go to a table immediately.

Saul points to a table in the corner. "That's the only one that's free," he says.

He pulls out the chair for me and I'm grateful. I slide my crutches under the table and sit down.

Miss Cassie claps her hands and calls out above our chatter. "Okay, tonight we're going to work with clay."

R.J. leans towards me from the next table and whispers, "Last week we used food and I made a meat pie...solid and good looking on the outside, but tasty and satisfying on the inside."

I let out a snort and laugh. He's funny. He grins,

and when Miss Cassie frowns, he smiles sweetly at her and I can't help laughing again. She frowns at me and I mutter, "Sorry." She smiles at me.

"Okay, you all know what you have to do. The purpose of this class is to express yourself and your feelings. You can do anything you want to with your clay. There are no rules, just be yourself and be honest."

The kids all begin to talk at once and the room is filled with noise, but within minutes they become silent as they all concentrate on the lump of clay in front of them.

What am I to do with mine? I glance around; everyone's busy. I need to make a start but what shall I make? How do I see myself and what am I feeling? I'm not sure I can do this. To make anything means that I have to acknowledge my feelings about myself, and about what's happening to me. I'm not sure that I'm ready to do that, but as all the kids around me are busying themselves with their clay, their hands sticky and brown, I make a start.

I suddenly feel hot as my thoughts drift. I used to be a person, one that knew what I was and who I was, but now I feel as if I have no real form. Everything changed for me when Tom died.

I look at the lump of clay and touch it with one finger. It's sticky and wet. I press my finger into it and the indentation stays there, showing me that I can make this lump of nothing into something if I only try.

Should I try and make an image of myself or should I make it into a deep pit, one that will show everyone the extent of my pain? No, a pit is just too easy; all I have to do is to punch a hole in the clay with my fist...that might feel good though.

I could smash the clay with both my fists to express the anger I feel that I should have to deal with all this pain when I'm just a kid. I didn't ask for it, and I'd give anything to make it go away, but that seems too easy. I want to do something with this lump of "me" other than smashing it with my fists.

I glance around and everyone is concentrating on the form their clay is taking. I take a deep breath in, hold it for as long as I can and then exhale slowly, allowing my feelings to take over me.

As I place my hands over the lump of wet clay, my head starts to swim and I feel as if I'm drifting and I'm only vaguely aware of the wet stickiness seeping through my fingers and dribbling down my wrists. I exert pressure through my hands and try to feel what's inside of me so that I can transport it to the clay before me. I feel as if I've disappeared somewhere and the room seems to fade away as I'm lost in a world where there's only me, my pain and the cool wet stickiness beneath my hands. Even though I have no plan, my fingers caress the clay and begin to shape it, and the sticky mess embeds itself under my nails...

It seems as if we've been in the room for all eternity and I'm jolted back into my seat when Miss Cassie calls out, "Okay, let's see what you've made."

I feel weird; like I've been on a journey where there was only me, and my only companion was my pain. I shake my head in an attempt to orient myself. I feel awful and long to get out of the room. I don't want to share any of this with anyone, but once again I can't do anything because I can't make a quick getaway. I know someone would stop me as I lurched awkwardly on my crutches towards the door, so I save myself the embarrassment and just stare out of the window.

My stomach churns with panic as I hear the kids explain their "creations" to Miss Cassie. She's getting nearer to me.

My face is burning with anxiety when she stops beside me, but she responds differently to how I imagine she would.

She says, "Oh my."

There's silence in the room; everyone's staring at me. I don't know what to say.

Miss Cassie shatters the silence by saying, "Adam, where did you learn to do that? I can't believe it. This is beautiful, truly beautiful. Will you tell everyone what this sculpture means?"

When she says the word "sculpture" I look at the lump of clay in front of me and suddenly I'm amazed. Before me is a figure, one hunched in agony. I feel shocked and surprised. Did I do this? Surely not, but as I look at my hands the proof lies under my nails.

Everyone's looking at me waiting to hear what I have to say. I cough to clear my throat and to give me a few seconds to think.

"Um, I, uh..." I don't know what to say. My face is burning, and I feel as if I'm stripped naked. No one rescues me, not even when I glance at Saul. He sits there staring at my "creation." What's the big deal? I just made a figure, that's all.

Miss Cassie says, "Adam, you are obviously very talented..."

I'm surprised. I've never thought of myself as talented in anything.

"...Your figure is *so* expressive," she says, falling silent.

Chelsea sees my embarrassment and speaks out.

"You don't have to explain the feelings your figure represents. I think we get it." She glances around the room and one by one the kids say, "Yeah."

Miss Cassie says, "Well, what are the feelings you see depicted in Adam's figure?"

The kids call out and they describe exactly how I'm feeling.

"Desperation."

"Depression."

"Hopelessness."

"Agony."

"Despair."

"Devastation."

"Being inconsolable."
"Feeling tormented."
"Being tortured."

My face is burning and I wish they'd stop, because everything they say describes exactly what I'm feeling. Their honesty leaves me nowhere to hide, and I feel stripped naked.

Chapter Eight

Miss Cassie tells me that she's going to put the figure in the kiln and she seems excited. I suppose I should be, too, but I'm not. I'm a bit surprised that I can sculpt, since I've never tried it before; it just sort of happened. I'm not sure what surprises me more: That I can do it so well or that other people can't. I'm shocked at being faced with an image of what my pain looks like; no wonder I feel so bad.

I go to bed early to get away from Holly and Nancy, who seem to be paying me even more attention since Miss Cassie liked my figure. As I lie staring at the ceiling, thoughts race around my head.

How is it that you can get to my age and not know that you're really good at something, yet you can do it just as if you've practiced for years? That's weird. It makes me wonder if I'd be good at other things I've never tried to do. What if I'd never tried to make something with clay? I'd never have found out that I could do it so well. Perhaps I should try to do other new things.

I turn over and try to get comfortable but my head is too busy thinking, so I turn over again. I'm troubled by what I've made. There's something horrible about the figure, something that scares me. When I truly looked at it after the kids had left the room, I could understand why they had shouted out all those different feelings, for each one was exactly how I'm feeling, and it showed in the figure. It feels overwhelming to know that so many awful feelings live inside me, and I don't know what to do with them all.

I toss and turn all night.

At breakfast Chelsea sits next to me.

"You were amazing last night," she says.

I shrug, not knowing what to say.

"I wish I could make something so beautiful."

I look at her and frown. "I don't think it's beautiful. I think it's hideous."

"You're kidding," she says, as if she can't believe what I've just said. She shakes her head. "No, you're wrong. It's beautiful, really beautiful."

I stuff a sausage into my mouth because I have the strongest urge to cuss at her. How can she believe that the pain inside me—for that's what the figure represents—is beautiful?

"You captured everything that's painful about

grief. It's awesome; you're awesome."

She leaves the table before I can chew the sausage and swallow. R.J. takes Chelsea's seat and sits at the table with a plate full of eggs, bacon and pancakes in front of him.

"How come you went to bed early last night? You missed a good evening. It was fun."

I feel a flash of sarcasm flow through me as I think, *Glad you were having fun while I was hurting so badly*, but I like him so I say nothing and stab another sausage with my fork. Saul joins us.

"Did you see Holly last night?" he whispers. "Hey, she can really move."

"What did I miss?" I ask.

Saul's got a big grin on his face. "The girls were practicing a dance routine. You should have been there, man."

So he was having fun, too, while I was hurting so badly. I don't know what to think. How can you be grieving and still have fun? I don't get it.

I follow them out of the dining room and, rather than go to the Group Room, we go back to Miss Cassie's room. I pray that the figure isn't anywhere around, because I don't think I can face it today and be reminded of all those awful things living inside me.

The room looks different, as the tables have been moved. On every table there's a checkerboard, with the pieces stacked alongside it.

Miss Cassie smiles as we walk through the door and tells us to sit around the big table. She sits at the head of the table and waits for us all to settle down.

"Today we are not going to dwell on feelings in this class, but we're going to focus upon thinking. We're going to look at life, and at death, and we're going to try and see it from a different perspective. That means that you are going to use your brains in order to think. Okay?"

I shift in my seat wondering what she's talking about.

"Who can tell me what the word 'certainty' means?"

A kid shouts out, "It's gonna happen no matter what."

Miss Cassie laughs and says, "Yes, you've got it. Something is going to happen regardless of anything you do."

I shift in my seat; where's she going with this?

"Who can give me examples of some certainties in life?" she asks.

R.J. laughs and says, "If you've got bad breath no one's gonna want to kiss you."

Everyone laughs, and so does Miss Cassie until she holds up her hand and tries to look serious. "What is the one certainty in life?"

She looks around the table, and all the kids are quiet. A couple of kids cough when the silence becomes heavy. I wrack my brain to think of an answer. There must be loads of things that are a certainty in life. If I had continued to drive without a license, I'd have been caught by the police. If I skip school, I won't graduate. I glance around the room.

Miss Cassie speaks for us. "The one certainty in life is that we are all going to die at some time. We don't know when or what the circumstances will be, but we *know* that we *will* die."

I shift in my seat.

"When you're young, dying seems so far off, and unless someone close to you dies, you may never give it a thought until you're much older. Believe me, when you get older, you'll think about it a lot more, not from a depressive point of view, but from the perspective of trying to make sense of your life and your place in the world. As I get older I wonder whether I'm going to have enough time left to finish all the things I've started," she says, grinning. "All those unfinished projects..."

"Doesn't it scare you?" Nancy asks, frowning at her. "It scares me."

Miss Cassie looks thoughtful for a moment, and then says, "I don't think I'm scared of dying; it's more the way I die that scares me. No one wants to die painfully. When I think about dying, I feel very sad because the thought of leaving the people I love seems intolerable to me...I think that's where my dread of dying comes from."

Everyone's quiet, and she seems to shake herself from her thoughts.

"Of course, your attitude towards death depends a lot upon your beliefs about whether there's an afterlife of some sort. Most religions teach that there is some form of life after death, although they differ in their perception of it, but you know, no one really knows what to expect. Faith really helps prepare you for your death and helps you through the grieving process, too."

Saul speaks out, "Yeah, but what if you don't believe in life after death? My family doesn't. They say, 'When you're dead, you're dead, that's it.'"

"What do you believe?" Miss Cassie asks him.

He shrugs. "I'm not sure. I can't believe this is all there is. What would be the point of it all? Why would everything hurt so much if it was all for nothing?"

"That's an interesting thing to say. Do you see pain as some form of penance?"

"What do you mean?" he frowns at her.

"Well, you make it sound as if enduring pain is the route to some sort of reward."

We all look at him and he shifts uncomfortably.

"Well, isn't that what the crucifixion is all about... pain on earth and a reward in heaven? Isn't that what all religions preach?"

Miss Cassie smiles ruefully at him, and says, "I think you may be right."

Chelsea speaks out. "I think it would be terrible

to lose someone you love if you don't believe in life after death. How do people who don't believe in life after death manage to get through the grieving process? It must be twice as bad."

"Why?"

"Because even though you miss the one you've lost, at least you can tell yourself that you'll see that person again, but if you don't believe...well...how can you have any hope?" She shrugs, and shakes her head as if she can't imagine how awful that would be.

I had never thought about life after death before Tom died, but since that awful Saturday evening every part of me has prayed that there is such a thing, for I can't bear the thought of never seeing him again.

Miss Cassie steers the conversation back towards what she has to say.

"I think there's no doubt that having some form of religious belief does help, first, to help the dying person come to terms with the end of their life, and second, it certainly helps the bereaved person go through the stages of the grieving process. But that doesn't mean that those who have no religious belief are doomed to stay stuck in the grieving process with no way out. It depends on so many things—how close they were to the one that died, or whether they felt any guilt about the death.

"Different cultures have different attitudes towards death. In some cultures a set amount of time is put aside for a public display of grieving where everyone howls and sobs loudly, but when that time is over, they get on with life without looking back."

R.J. grins. "I like that," he says.

"It can be a very positive way to get your emotions out," Miss Cassie says. "So often people get embarrassed when they see someone crying, or they don't know what to say, so they avoid speaking to the person who's bereaved. In the end the bereaved person ends up trying to make other people feel less awkward, and so they bottle their feelings up and may stay stuck in the grieving process. Many cultures are so much better than us at dealing with death."

"My biggest fear as a little kid," Holly blurts out, "was to see a dead body. It used to give me nightmares."

"You see dead bodies all the time in my neighborhood," one kid says, frowning. "It seems like every weekend someone is shot or stabbed."

I look at him and there's something weary about his face that tells me he knows more about pain than I do.

Silence hangs in the air for a moment and we all look to Miss Cassie to break it.

"Okay, so we accept that no one knows for certain whether there is some form of life after death, and we recognize that most religions are based on the belief of an afterlife. But what about your beliefs about *life*?"

"What d'you mean?" several kids ask.

She smiles at us, and I know that she's about to force my brain to work.

"Well, if you believe that there's an afterlife, what are you doing here? Is there a purpose to your life here on earth? Are you here for a reason? Think about these things. There are no absolute answers, no right or wrong answers, but you need to think about these questions, because the way that you think will impact the way you grieve the loss of the people you love."

I feel a bit lost and I sit in silence, as do most of the others.

Miss Cassie looks around at us, and says, "Okay, how about we look at life in a different way. What if there is some form of afterlife and a form of 'higher being,' some people might call that being 'God,' that wants us to grow and learn. Could your presence here on earth be in order to learn something? If there is life *after* death, could there be life *before* life?"

Everyone is very quiet.

"What if...what if you had to learn something specific; it would make sense to be born into an environment where you could learn that specific thing. For example, if you're at school and have to take a science class, you wouldn't go to an English class and expect to learn science; you'd have to go to a science class to learn science."

Everyone's frowning including me.

Miss Cassie smiles and clears her throat.

"What if *you* choose the type of life you're going to live so that while on earth you will have the opportunity to learn whatever it is that you have to learn?"

We're still very quiet.

"Y'know, when I was a teenager, I was really mad at my parents. I was mad at the world and mad at God. Every time something went wrong I would shout at my parents, "I didn't ask to be born," trying to make them feel bad for the bad things that were happening to me. I was ready to blame everyone for the pain in my life. But one day someone said, 'What if living on earth is like going to school? You choose what it is that you have to learn and then choose where you're most likely to learn that lesson.'"

Everyone is listening.

"Think about it. If you were to learn about poverty, you wouldn't choose to be born into a wealthy family. If you were to learn how to help people, choosing a family where you'd experience a lot of pain would help you to achieve lessons in life far more than if you chose to live in a family with no problems.

"When I changed the way I thought, I suddenly lost the anger I felt towards my parents, society and God. I was actually thankful that I'd experienced all the things that I'd found painful, because perhaps, just perhaps—and no one knows—I am learning what I'm meant to learn in my life. When I changed the way I saw my life, my attitude changed. That's what I mean by, 'What are your beliefs about life?' We ask ourselves whether there's life after death, but what if there's life before life?"

My head is beginning to spin as she's talking. Did Tom come to this earth for a reason that I know nothing about, and was his death meant to be? Am I here for some specific reason? Did I choose to be born into my family? The thought is appalling to me. No one in their right mind would choose to be born into my family; but what if I had? What lesson would I be bound to learn by being in my family? It comes to me in a flash...I could help children just like I try to help my younger brothers, and losing Tom and going through the grieving process, I think I could help others who have lost someone. I also know what it feels like to be in such pain that you don't want to live anymore...perhaps I could stop people from committing suicide. My head is spinning in circles as thoughts cascade through me, but I feel really alive and it feels good.

"When you learn about science and psychology, you will see that nothing is really as it seems. All we have with which to make sense of the life we live is our human brains, and they are limited. There are things in this universe that we cannot hope to understand because our human brains cannot make sense of them. I believe that the parables in the Bible are stories that help us to understand something that our human brains are unlikely to understand if put another way. If we recognize our limitations as human beings, then we can accept that there are things beyond our comprehension, and death and any form of an afterlife are included in those things."

"I don't get it," a kid says.

"Don't worry, this isn't easy," Miss Cassie says. "Let me tell you about an experiment researchers did years ago to explore how the environment impacts the brain."

This sounds interesting.

"Scientists built a large, round drum that had thick vertical lines painted inside it. Several newborn kittens were placed inside the empty drum the moment they were born, away from their mothers."

"Oh, that's cruel," Holly says.

"Yes, it was, but they did it anyway," Miss Cassie continues. "The only thing those kittens saw were vertical stripes, and their brain cells, used to only seeing vertical lines, only registered vertical lines. They grew bigger believing that their world only consisted of things shaped with vertical lines, even though we all know that the world consists of horizontal, diagonal and curved lines, too. The experimenters finally let the kittens out into a normal room and they bumped into every object in front of them that had horizontal, diagonal and curved lines.

The kittens' brains just hadn't developed to be able to see anything other than vertical lines. They were able to avoid all the chair legs because they were vertical and they could 'see' them, but they were blind to anything that had horizontal lines, like the bottom of a door, or a ball with circular lines, and they walked straight into them."

Everyone is deadly quiet and my brain is working overtime trying to make sense of what she's saying, and how it might apply to me.

"All the experimenters could see everything in the room by using their brains, but the kittens couldn't. So, what if...what if our human brains don't *see* everything that's *really* out there? What if we're like those kittens with limited ability to see what's truly out there? It's an amazing thought, isn't it? We are limited by our human brains; we see only what they allow us to see, and that thought sets me free. It enables me to leave the argument alone about what life is or isn't, or what death is or isn't, because I don't believe that I have the necessary tools to be able to work it out. My understanding is limited by my human brain, just like the kittens whose brains developed according to the world they were in."

No one says a word, and I feel like I'm thinking for myself for the first time in my life. I've never thought about life or death in these ways before, and although it's a bit scary, I like it. It makes me feel more alive than I've ever felt in my whole life.

Saul glances at me and whispers under his breath, "Wow."

"One of the things I love about the Bible is that it uses everyday events to try and illustrate its messages. If you look hard enough, you can find lessons in most of the things around us, and those lessons help us to understand life and death as best we can."

I feel sceptical because I'm not sure what she means.

She breaks into my thoughts. "Who can play checkers?"

Everyone puts their hand up and starts to talk, breaking the awkward silence.

"Okay, let's look at a game of checkers and see what it can teach us about life and death."

She opens a checkerboard in front of her and asks two kids next to her to put the pieces on the right squares.

"Okay, try to imagine that this board represents your life-span, be it an hour or a hundred years. The one certainty in life is that you are going to die one day. The one certainty in a game of checkers is that it *will* come to an end, just like life. Let's imagine that one of the pieces is you and the other pieces are the people who come in and out of your life; they may be people you know or they may be strangers. The moves you make as the game goes on are your path through life.

"Just like life, when you play a game of checkers

you work out what move to make next, or sometimes you just move anywhere without too much thought or planning. Let's imagine that when the pieces are 'taken,' it represents the death of a person in your life; again it may be a person who you know well or it may be a stranger. But still it is a person who exists in your lifetime and their death may impact your life in ways that you can't imagine, or don't realize. I want you each to pair up and begin to play checkers, and think about what I've just said."

Saul helps me to my feet and grabs my crutches. We sit at the nearest table and he tosses a coin to see who's going to start first. He wins.

Miss Cassie walks around the room, as each game begins, and watches us play. Saul moves a piece and so do I, and then he moves another. I look into his eyes to try and fathom what his plan is, and he grins at me. I'm hopeless at this, and I hope he can't see it in my face. I make my move and he yells out, "Yes," then jumps over two of my pieces and lands on my side of the board, two moves away from getting a "king." I'm embarrassed because everyone looks over at us and I think they can see my shame.

Miss Cassie holds her hand up and tells us all to stop so that we can listen.

"Okay, at this point in the game, or rather, at this point in your life-span, two pieces have been 'taken' because you moved in a certain direction. I bet you are sitting there thinking, 'What if I'd moved that piece in the other direction? Then he wouldn't have "taken" my two pieces.' I want you all to concentrate for a moment and think about 'what ifs.' All of you have experienced losing a loved one, so how many of you have thought, 'What if I'd done something different? Perhaps my loved one would still be alive.'"

A shiver trickles down my back as I think "what ifs" every minute of every day, and have done so since Tom died. What if I hadn't asked him to drive me to Becky's; what if I had called her father and left Tom at the hospital when Kelly was having surgery; what if I hadn't been going out with Becky.

"Look at the game before you. Yes, you can probably work out a move that would have prevented a particular piece from being 'taken' right this minute, but remember, the one certainty in a game of checkers is that it will end with most if not all the pieces having been 'taken.'"

I'm trying to make sense of what she's saying, and it's becoming clearer.

"Remember the one certainty in life is that we are all going to die. Whether one person dies early in your life-span or later does not alter the end result, which is that in a hundred years everyone that's alive in your lifetime will be dead. The checkers game's the same—when it's over, all the pieces will no longer be on the board."

I think I see what she means.

"I think the hardest thing to understand about this analogy...Does everyone know what an analogy is?"

I shake my head as Chelsea speaks. "Is it a picture to explain something that's hard to understand?"

"Yes, more or less. It's when you liken something that's hard to understand to something else that's easy to understand in order to help you understand something complex. Does that make sense?"

I nod and others say, "Yes."

"Well, I think the hardest thing to understand about this analogy is that the pattern the checker pieces make on the board changes depending upon the decisions you make during the game. You will sit there and say, 'What if I had moved to this square or that square; then I wouldn't have lost that piece,' just as you might dwell on 'what ifs' in real life. You may beat yourself up by saying, 'What if I had done this or that differently; then I wouldn't have lost that person in my life.' The choices you make *will* change the matrix of your life. But there is one inescapable fact, and that is...we are all going to die one day, no matter what we do or don't do. The checkers game is going to end one way or another whether you lose one particular piece early on in the game, or later in the game. The different pattern the pieces make due to the different decisions you make and the different moves you make will make no difference to the end result. The game will end. It's the same in life. Your life on earth is going to end one day, and what you do or don't do, although it may change the lives of the people who live during your life-span, is not going to change that fact."

Is she trying to tell me that what I did or didn't do on that Saturday makes no difference to whether Tom died? Is she trying to tell me that, if he hadn't died that day, he might have died another day under different circumstances? I understand that we are all going to die one day, but is she trying to tell me that, depending upon whether we are in the wrong place at the wrong time, we'll be snatched from this life just like the two checker pieces Saul has "taken" from the checkerboard in front of us? Is she saying that it is of no real consequence when a person dies, either early or late in their lives? Surely not; I can't believe that.

"What do you think?" she asks us.

R.J. sounds angry. "Are you saying that life is just a game?"

"Absolutely not. The game of checkers is just an analogy to help you understand that all life comes to an end, just as all checkers games come to an end. Whether one piece is 'taken' from the board early or late in the game, it does not alter the fact that the game will end. Life is definitely not a game. The loss of one person *will* change the dynamics of those left behind, and different choices, or moves, will be made because of that loss, but the end result will be the same—our time on earth will end."

"But your analogy doesn't take into account the pain people feel when they lose someone. It's very different to being 'taken' in a checkers game and losing your pieces; it isn't as cold blooded in real life. Losing someone hurts," Chelsea says wisely.

"Absolutely," Miss Cassie says. "I agree with you, but remember, I said that today we were going to look at thinking about things in a different way; we weren't going to consider feelings. I wanted you all to be able to explore the way you think about life and death, and to help you get rid of any blame or guilt that you may harbor. Things happen for a reason, and that reason may not be clear to you now, and may never be, but try to accept that life is working out the way it's supposed to, even if you don't understand it right this minute. Analogies like this help you to grasp something that is virtually impossible to understand with our limited human brains. All we can do is try to find a belief that will ease our pain and make sense to us. We can explore our beliefs about death and also about life, and why we're here. All I can do is to tell you what helps me, for there are no right or wrong answers. No one can truly know for sure about life and death, and that's what makes it so hard to understand. You have to work it out for yourself and accept what feels right for you."

Everyone is silent.

"I've tried to show you that there may be things bigger than the life we see here on earth with our limited brains, things that we have little hope of really understanding. What you have to do is to find a way of thinking and seeing things that makes it okay in your head and heart. For me, it was to believe that existence on earth resembles some type of 'school,' the purpose of which is to learn something that *I* have chosen; something that I need to learn. Believing in this helps me to stop feeling sorry for myself when times get rough, and it also gives me courage that tells me I can cope when life hurts."

She looks around at us to make sure we're all listening, and we are.

"It also gives me something else. If I believe that I've *chosen* the life I live in order to learn something that is important enough for me to be here in this life, then to commit suicide when life gets tough and I'm in pain means that I've failed in what I'm here to learn. If I think in this way, then the thought of ending my life before I've learned what I'm here to learn is unthinkable. Who can guess why?"

Everyone's quiet, in fact, no one moves. I rack my brains to think of the answer. If I am here in this life-span merely to learn something and I fail, what will happen?

Suddenly I think of Jed who messed up a couple

of classes last year...he had to retake that year.

I venture to break the silence that fills the room as Miss Cassie looks around at everyone who's staring at the floor.

"You'll have to retake the class...I mean, you'll have to come back again to learn the lesson you chose to learn."

Miss Cassie smiles at me and makes me feel like a million dollars.

"Yes, absolutely right. If this way of thinking about life and death is right and you have struggled throughout your life—suffered terrible pain while trying to follow your destiny—the thought of failing and having to come back to endure all that pain again is dreadful. No one in their right mind would commit suicide, if only for that reason."

I shiver even though a warm breeze comes through the open window. I couldn't bear to have to go through the pain I've felt since Tom died, and in this instant when Miss Cassie opens her mouth to start speaking again, I make a promise to myself. *No matter how bad life gets, I will never end my life, for the thought of having to retake this class called "Life" is too awful to imagine. I vow to plod on to the end, no matter how hard or how painful it is.*

Miss Cassie looks at us and says, "Okay, carry on with your game of checkers and good luck." She goes quiet for a brief moment and something flashes across her face. She smiles at us and says, "Hey guys, this is a tough thing to look at, and I think you're all awesome."

Chapter Nine

Miss Cassie lets us go and we sit outside in the sun. I'm frustrated when I see most of the kids head for the beach and I know I can't go. I'd give anything to be able to stand at the edge of the water and skim stones. I'm grateful when Saul and R.J. sit with me on the grass at the edge of the playground.

"That was a bit heavy," Saul says, putting his shades on.

Chelsea joins us and smiles at me.

"Do you think we're alive to learn something, Adam?" she asks me, pointedly.

I shrug. I really don't know. As I look out to sea it all seems to look different, and I wonder if I'll ever look at life in the same way again.

"I don't know. Why is everything so hard? I thought adults had the answers, but all Miss Cassie's done is to show me that there aren't any real answers, and we've got to work it out for ourselves."

"Yeah," R.J. says, "it would be good if adults could give us a fact sheet saying exactly what life's all about, what death really is and what happens after we die. Y'know, adults suck. They expect you to do everything they want because 'they know best,' and yet when you're faced with something as painful as losing someone you love, they don't know anything, and they tell us we have to work it out for ourselves."

He's got a point.

"Yes, but we're not talking about things that have any real concrete answers," Chelsea says. "We're talking about things that Miss Cassie says our human brains can't truly understand. That's different, isn't it?"

"Maybe there are no answers," I say, trying to sound smart.

Saul lies back on the grass and says, "Maybe I'm too young to work my limited brain so hard."

I laugh and so does R.J., but Chelsea doesn't.

"I liked what Miss Cassie said about choosing what you come here to learn, because that implies that everyone is on a mission and when it's over it's time to leave this life..."

She falls silent for a moment before continuing.

"...Let's imagine that it's true, then when someone dies, we shouldn't feel any kind of guilt or blame...in fact, perhaps we should be pleased for them."

Saul sits up.

"Do what? You think that we should be *pleased* when someone we love dies?"

She suddenly sounds excited, as if she's found the last piece of a jigsaw she's been working on for years.

"Well, of course you won't be *pleased*, because it hurts to lose someone you love. But if you can see it from a different perspective, it might change the way you *feel* about it."

Saul takes his shades off and polishes them in his tee-shirt, squinting at her as she continues talking.

"Listen, my cousin just finished college. She decided when she was my age that she wanted to go to veterinarian school. It's all she's ever wanted to do, and she worked really hard to keep her grades up. It's really hard to get into vet school, and you wouldn't believe what she went through to get a place. Even after she was accepted, she spent years studying, got soaked to the skin attending sick animals out in the fields, had her arms up to the elbows in poop, and battled self-doubt all the time. Think about how happy she was when she graduated. She was ecstatic; she'd achieved what she'd set out to do, she'd learned what she'd set out to learn. Even though we knew that once she graduated she would move away, we were really happy for her, and we had a massive party to celebrate. It was cool."

Saul puts his polished shades back on, and with a

grin on his face that tells me he got what she's trying to say but is playing with her, says, "And your point is?"

She doesn't seem to notice; she's so animated.

"She was on a mission to learn how to become a vet. That's what she had decided to learn. Even though it was hard, she never gave up; and once she graduated, she moved away and we rarely saw her, and we missed her. Isn't that the same as what Miss Cassie has been trying to tell us about coming to this life to learn something? Think about it! If someone has learned what they came to learn, shouldn't we be pleased? And if there *is* an afterlife, then the person who's died would be pleased with what they've achieved."

R.J. laughs at her, but not unkindly.

"You're beginning to sound like Miss Cassie."

Irritation flashes across her face.

"Sometimes, R.J., you can be such a jerk," and she jumps up and storms off.

"What did I do?" he shrugs.

"Y'know, she's got a point," Saul says.

"What, that I'm a jerk?"

We laugh.

"No, idiot," he says. "Think about what she's just said. It's pretty awesome. You *would* be pleased if you achieved what you set out to learn. I like what she said about her cousin struggling and surviving years of hard work to become a vet. That's the same as surviving all the crappy things that happen to you in life. Work it out. She said that after her cousin graduated and moved away, they rarely saw her again and they all missed her. Isn't that the same as the grief people feel when someone dies? The person who has died is just fine, especially if they've learned what they set out to learn. It's those who are left behind who hurt and suffer because they miss the person who died, just as Chelsea missed her cousin who moved away. It makes perfect sense to me. We just have to find a way to deal with missing the person who has died, that's all."

"Just like that!" R.J. grins.

"Yeah, just like that. Hey, it's too hot out here. Let's go and get a soda and find Chelsea," Saul says, getting up and offering me his hand.

Chelsea's slumped in one of the squashy chairs in the family room and refuses to look up at us as we come through the door, but she giggles when R.J. dives on her, digging her in the ribs.

"Don't get all moody on us," he says playfully. "We think you're pretty smart. You made everything Miss Cassie said easy to understand."

"Yeah, we decided that all we have to do to crack this grieving process thing is to find a way to cope with missing the person who's died," Saul says, throwing me a soda which I just barely catch.

Ken appears in the doorway.

"Hey, Adam, you've got visitors."

I hobble after him on my crutches towards the visitation room, wondering who's come to see me. Mom stands up as Ken opens the door, and suddenly from behind one of the chairs is a squeal, and Kelly all but knocks me over. Mom comes over and tries to put her arms around me.

"How are you, Adam? We miss you so much. How's your leg? Are they feeding you enough? You look pale. Are you getting enough sleep?" she says all at once.

Kelly clings to my good leg and makes me laugh. I feel as if my heart is going to burst, and I suddenly realize how much I've missed her. Mom takes her off me so that I can sit down, but as soon as I'm seated she scrambles up onto my good leg and soaks my face with wet, sloppy kisses.

Mom tells me that the boys are driving her crazy, but that Jed is helping her. Sherrie is as mean as ever, especially since she split up with Jason after a huge fight, and Nancy is doing better now that she's out of the hospital.

"How come she hasn't come to visit me?" I ask, fearing that she still blames me for Tom's death.

"She wanted to, Adam, but she's ashamed of the way she behaved and is anxious about facing you. She asked me to give this to you."

She hands me a letter and my stomach lurches. I don't want to read it in front of Mom, so I stuff it in my pocket.

Kelly tries to stuff a piece of candy into my mouth and makes me laugh.

"How's her leg?" I ask, looking at Kelly as she wriggles on my good leg.

"It's fine. Kelly, show Uncle Adam your boo boo."

She slides off me and sits on the floor, taking her shoes off and begins tugging at her socks.

"Look," she says proudly, and shows me a fresh scar. "It's all better now and doesn't hurt anymore." She jumps up and runs around the room yelling, then charges at me and clambers back onto my lap.

"Yes, she's better," I say to Mom, who smiles at me.

She seems different—not so angry or annoyed.

"What's wrong?" I ask.

She looks flustered. "Nothing. I've been worried about you, that's all."

"I'm fine. It's cool here. They've really helped me to see things differently."

"That's good," she says, suddenly sounding awkward, as if she doesn't want to talk about anything that will make her feel uncomfortable. I guess we don't talk in our family; we should. But I remember what Miss Cassie said about people not knowing how to deal with someone who's grieving, so I don't feel badly towards Mom. That's just how she is.

Kelly distracts us from an awkward silence, and we watch her trying to put her socks back on and laugh as she gets her shoes on the wrong feet.

When they leave, Mom hugs me and says that she can't wait until I come home, and she mutters a quick apology for screaming at me for drinking her whiskey. I tell her that I did wrong and she had every right to be mad at me. Kelly starts to cry when she realizes that they are leaving, but Miss Tina makes her smile by giving her one of the balloons that represent Ken's brain.

I feel weird watching them go. Something's different about my mom, and I don't know what it is.

"Good visit?" Miss Tina asks as I limp down the hall towards the playground doors.

"Yeah, not bad. Better than I expected."

"Oh, why's that?"

I stop and lean against the wall with a frown upon my face.

"My mom seemed different somehow."

"In what way?"

I think hard. "I don't know. She was softer, more quiet, not so angry or harsh." Miss Tina doesn't say anything. "She's always shouting." I shake my head and shrug. "She just seems different."

"The death of someone in the family can change people in different ways. We can only guess what effect Tom's death has had upon her. I know that she has been worried about you and your sister, that's for sure. Maybe she's done some thinking, some soul searching...who knows? Was that your niece?"

I can't help but grin. I feel a bit embarrassed. It

doesn't seem very cool to be so crazy about a three-year-old kid, but I am. "Yes, I've babysat her since she was born and we're very close."

Miss Tina pats my arm and smiles at me.

"That's wonderful," she says. "You're both very lucky to have each other. See you in group in a minute, okay?"

I grab a soda and go to the Group Room where the others are already seated. Miss Tina walks into the room and everyone stops talking.

"Miss Cassie tells me that you've been working on some pretty heavy stuff. Who has something to say?"

I see Saul, R.J. and Chelsea glance at each other, and Saul breaks the silence.

"Well, we worked out that all we have to do to crack this grieving process thing is to find a way to cope with missing the person who's died," Saul says, and the others nod.

Miss Tina laughs. "You make it sound so simple, so easy."

"Well, that's what we think," R.J. says, grinning at her.

"Say more," she says.

Chelsea takes over. "Well, we thought that if you were able to feel good about the memories of the one you've lost, then they won't really have gone...they'll still live in your heart and will always be there, even if they aren't there physically."

Miss Tina nods slowly, taking in what they're saying. She smiles.

"Well, that brings me to a story I want to read to you about exactly that. One of the secrets to getting through grief is to be able to find yourself in place where you can smile at your memories of the one you've lost, for you haven't really lost them. Those we love live in our hearts and in our memories, so you can feel the love you shared just by thinking about them and enjoying your memories."

"Are you ready?" she asks, and everyone's quiet.

• • • •

Far, far away in the land that bobbed in and out of view depending upon the sea mist, deep within the forest lived a woodcutter. All his life he had lived in the forest and had learned from his father the ways of the trees. As a boy he spent from dawn to dusk with his father who showed him how to tend the young saplings. And as he grew older the young trees grew into fine, strong, upright boughs that soared upwards to reach the sun.

When the trees had grown tall, he learned from his father how to fell the trees to make a house and to carve fine furniture, but always they replanted fresh young saplings to replace the trees they cut down. The woodcutter learned to respect the trees for their beauty and for the livelihood they offered.

His father also taught him to grow and tend vines, and he marvelled at how different each one was. There was ivy growing all over their wooden house and grapevines growing in rows beneath the hot sun. He learned to pick the ripe fruit from the vines, and as the sun went down, his father would laugh as he pulled off his socks and began to stomp on the fruit until it was ready to make into wine. Life was good for the young woodcutter and his father.

One day when they were deep within the forest, a storm came upon them and darkness fell. The young woodcutter was not afraid as he followed his father, but in the dim light they lost their way.

"Where are we?" he asked his father, but the old man looked uncertain.

"It must be this way," he said, plowing through the branches in the dimness. But as the forest became thicker and the darkness grew, his father said, "Let's rest here until the clouds pass."

When the light returned, they stood up and brushed the leaves from their clothes.

"Let's go this way," the old man said, but they had strayed so far from the paths they knew that they became even more lost—until they saw a shaft of light ahead.

As they made their way towards the light, the young woodcutter gasped in awe. They had stumbled into a circular clearing that was surrounded by tall trees, and each was covered in a vine with lilac flowers hanging all around them that shone in the sunlight like beautiful, pointed lanterns.

"What is it?" he asked his father.

"I've heard of this place," he cried. "It's the Sacred Circle, where the ancients came to pray for those who they had loved and lost. Those who came here were wistful."

"What's wistful?" his son asked.

"Those who were wistful were full of sadness and longing. They were melancholy and yearned for their pain to go away, so the Gods of the Trees gave the mere mortals a gift, something to remind them of the beauty in those people they had loved and lost. The Gods of the Trees called this beautiful vine 'Wisteria' after those who came to this sacred place feeling wistful but who left with their spirit gladdened by the beauty before them.

The young woodcutter and his father made their way home in the light, and the image of the Sacred Circle stayed in the young woodcutter's memories and in his dreams as he grew into a man.

Years later, when he had become a man, his father died, and in his loneliness he sought a wife. He cleaned his little wooden house and made new furniture from the trees he cut down. When his daughter was born he felt that his life was complete and that the Gods of the Trees were smiling upon him.

As soon as his daughter could walk, he showed

her how to plant saplings and, as she grew, he taught her everything his father had taught him about the trees in the forest. She loved the trees as he had, and like his father before him.

They lived in perfect harmony in the forest, and they knew peace. As her fifth birthday neared, her father declared that she was old enough to tend her own little garden, and he pegged out a small plot of land in front of their little wooden house. He stood with a sapling in each hand, smiling at her.

"You are old enough to take care of your own trees. Here, plant these, and every day you have to tend to them and you will enjoy them."

He helped her to dig two deep holes, and as she scooped the earth back over the roots of the trees, he smiled. She stood by each tree twice a day with a watering can that was almost as big as her, spraying drops of water onto the two little trees. They grew and flourished, and she was so excited when bright green leaves sprouted from their branches.

As they grew, so did she, and she was as happy as any small child could be, and the woodcutter's heart was full. One day, however, disease came upon the woodcutter's family and his daughter's trees. He fought to save his wife, but she was destined to live with the Gods of the Trees, and so she died.

A vicious storm settled over the forest and the wind howled, yet its howling was drowned by the wailing of the woodcutter and his daughter, whose pain was immeasurable. In the morning, after the storm had passed, the woodcutter's daughter ventured out into the garden to tend to her two trees with a heavy heart.

As she made her way down the garden path, her father heard her cry, "Nooooooo!" He rushed out to find her, forgetting to put his boots on, such was the agony in her voice. He stood by her side, and tears poured down her face as she stood before one of her trees, its leaves dead and shriveled.

"How can this have happened?" she sobbed. "I've treated both trees the same. Why would one tree live and the other die?"

The pain in his heart was unbearable, and her question echoed his own lament, "Why was he still alive when his wife wasn't? It made no sense." He didn't know how to answer his grief-stricken daughter.

She fell into a deep depression, one where she was saturated in sadness and longing, where she was steeped in melancholy and yearned for her pain to go away. As she sat staring at the withered dead tree, pain lodged in her heart. She longed for her mother and she longed for her tree, and she couldn't understand the loss of either.

The woodcutter did not know what to do. He wrung his hands and busied himself deep within the forest, tending to his trees and hacking off dead branches. He burned the logs on the fire at night in an attempt to keep his daughter and himself warm from the chilling grief that gripped their hearts. But no matter how many logs he put on the fire in their simple wooden house, their grief chilled them to the bone and they could find no comfort.

He despaired at the loneliness he saw in his beautiful daughter's face as she missed her mother and lamented over the death of her tree. She berated herself, asking what she had done wrong; why had the Gods of the Trees taken her mother, and why had they withered her tree when she had tended them equally? She was without answers and the pain in her heart grew. The woodcutter watched in despair as his daughter slipped further away from him, grief stricken.

One morning as she sat beneath the withered tree, ignoring the one that was flourishing, the pain in his heart was so terrible that he could not bear to watch her, so he set off into the forest. He wandered without destination—his only purpose was to get away from his own pain and hopelessness—when suddenly he was drawn to shafts of light ahead of him. He stumbled forward, a memory deep within him stirring. And there, all around him, was the Sacred Circle where those who were lost in grief came, a place that he had discovered with his father all those years ago.

The woodcutter fell to the forest floor and sobbed, praying for guidance from the Gods of the

Trees, as he cried for his father, his wife and his daughter. His cries echoed around the Sacred Circle, and the beautiful pointed lilac lanterns shimmered in the sunlight. As his cries subsided, a faltering peace came upon him.

A voice deep within him said, "I remember this. My memory of this place is wonderful and has never left me. As I sit here I feel as if my father is still with me, for I have my memories of us being here together, and when I think of them it's as if he's still with me and nothing can take that away from me."

He sat in the Sacred Circle surrounded by the shimmering pointed lilac lanterns, his memories alive in his mind, and as peace settled over him, he knew that nothing could take his father and wife away from him while their memories remained in his heart.

Suddenly, as if the Gods of the Trees had spoken to him, he jumped up, and with a prayer on his lips he cut three branches from the Wisteria that draped itself over the forest trees around the Sacred Circle like Christmas ornaments. He hurried home through the fading light and didn't stop until he reached the little wooden house deep within the forest. There he found his daughter, her eyes still red from weeping, and he grabbed her hand.

"Come with me," he urged, and ignored her despondency, tugging on her sleeve. She followed him outside into her little garden where the one tree flourished and the other had withered for no reason, and she watched her father. His excitement was infectious as he began to dig furiously at the soil surrounding the withered tree. She didn't understand but drew near anyway, her curiosity ignited.

The woodcutter didn't stop digging until he was satisfied, and only then did he fall back onto the grass and let out a sigh of satisfaction. His daughter didn't understand, and she wasn't sure how to react. Part of her wanted to shout and be angry, to continue to be angry with the one person who truly knew her pain and whose love was strong enough to withstand her raging, but another part of her was intrigued.

"What are you doing?" she asked, her voice tinged with irritation and anger, for she was being drawn towards understanding, a place that she was not ready to inhabit, yet he seemed insistent.

"It's hard to be faced with death all the time. You spend far more time with your dead tree than with the one that's living and flourishing. Every time you look out of the window or come to the garden you're faced with this barren, naked, withered tree, one that died for no reason that you or I can see. You treated them the same, yet for some reason unknown to us, one died. The sight of this tree, so withered and dead, hurts your heart, and so I know what to do."

The little girl wiped her nose on her sleeve, sniffed, but listened to her father.

"I have been to the Sacred Circle and have been given a gift, the gift of memories and peace."

He planted the Wisteria vines in the hole around the withered, dead tree and patted down the earth.

"We have to focus upon our memories of the ones we have lost, for they have never really left us if we have memories of them. These Wisteria vines come from the Sacred Circle to remind us that memories keep our loved ones alive in our hearts."

The woodcutter's daughter dried her eyes and listened to her father. "The Wisteria will remind us to focus upon our memories of the ones we've lost rather than their absence." He stood up and went to bed, his heart lighter than it had been since the day his wife died. His daughter followed him with doubt in her heart.

Two difficult years passed, but on the anniversary of her mother's death and the withering of her tree, the woodcutter's daughter stood in her little garden and smiled. There in front of her, covering every part of the dead and withered tree, was thick green foliage. The Wisteria, that represented the memories of those they had loved and lost, had entwined its way around the dead tree and had brought it "alive" again so that she could still enjoy the tree.

The woodcutter and his daughter smiled at each other, for even though each knew that the tree was dead, that his wife and her mother was dead, so they relished in their memories, which kept her "alive."

Years later, no one would have guessed that the second tree had died, for the Wisteria inhabited every part of its withered branches. People came from far and wide to see the exquisite pointed lilac lantern-shaped blooms that depicted the memories of the ones they had loved and lost.

The woodcutter and his daughter found peace in their trees and vines, but none offered the same peace that they found by watching the Wisteria, their memories bringing alive the dead and withered tree before them. They learned that, although their loved ones had withered and died physically, the memories of them kept them alive in their hearts, just as the Wisteria had brought to life the barren, dead branches of the tree that had for some un-known reason failed to live.

• • • •

Miss Tina looks up and Chelsea speaks out.

"Oh, Miss Tina, that was beautiful."

"Did you all understand its message?" she asks.

"Yes, I think so. The Sacred Circle was a place where you can find peace. That could be anywhere... right?"

"Yes, some people find peace in church, others in a garden...I find peace by the ocean," Miss Tina says.

Chelsea carries on, "And the fact that one of the two little trees died even though the woodcutter's daughter treated them both the same is like one person dying and another one living, even though their lives were the same."

"Yeah," I say, "like Tom dying and me living, even though we were in the same accident, and none of it making any sense."

Miss Tina nods at me.

"Then the Wisteria vines growing all over the dead tree," Chelsea continues, "make it seem as if it hadn't died at all. The Wisteria flowers are the beautiful memories of those who have died...which means that even though the person has died, just like the tree, you can still enjoy the person who's died by enjoying your memories of them. Is that right?"

She looks around at us all and then at Miss Tina.

Miss Tina smiles at her, and says, "I think you covered everything, Chelsea. Well, done."

"How did you think of that story?" Saul asks.

She smiles and says, "Well, I planted two trees, tended them exactly the same, and one died. It looked so barren in my garden, so I planted Wisteria all around it and then it looked beautiful and didn't look dead at all. It became the frame to support the Wisteria, and I thought about how those who have died can be a framework for our memories of them and how that would help us cope with missing them. Can thinking in this way help you cope with missing the one you've lost?"

She looks at Saul, and says, "You said, 'The way to crack this grieving process thing is to find a way to cope with missing the person who has died,' so do you think that focusing on your memories of the person rather than their absence will help you cope with missing them?"

Saul grins, and says, "I think so."

The kids nod, and so do I.

Chapter Ten

Miss Tina lets us go and I head for the bathroom. When I get outside the kids are on the beach, and again I feel envious. I sit on a swing feeling a bit sorry for myself; it's no fun breaking your leg.

I remember the letter from Nancy in my pocket and tear the envelope open. As I read, the noise of kids laughing and hanging out, and seagulls screeching above me, fades.

Dear Adam,

I don't know where to begin so I'll just start and hope it's at the right place. I don't know if you know this, but you've always been my favorite brother. I shouldn't have favorites, I know, but I can't help it. I know that life has been tough for you since Dad left, and Mom has expected you to be the man of the house. She's relied on you too much and I have, too...we all have. I hate that you've had to cope with Sherrie's moods; I know she picks on you and I feel bad that I haven't been there to fight in your corner.

I hated moving out when I married Tom because I felt as if I was abandoning you. You boys always looked so miserable when I came home. I'm sorry I wasn't there for you when Tom and I first got married. I know that you all loved him and that in some ways he made up for Dad leaving.

I know you're hurting now and I have made that harder for you by blaming you for Tom's death. I'm so sorry, Adam. I was crazy that night and I lost it. I'd give anything to take it back, but I can't. Please try and forgive me, please, babe.

None of it was your fault...I hope you'll believe me when I say that. Yes, you wanted to get to Becky's on time for her birthday surprise, but it was Tom's decision to drive you there and his decision to drive too fast. He didn't have to; he could have paid for a taxi to take you there, or he could have driven slowly, but he chose not to do those things. I hope you really hear me when I say that he chose to do those things...he didn't have to.

Yes, I was mad for a while that he chose to leave me with Kelly when she was about to go for surgery. I was scared, Kelly was scared and I needed him, but he chose to be the hero. I'm not being mean so don't be angry, but there are things that you don't know about Tom.

He loved to be the hero; he loved to be adored, and he would do anything for you boys but not much for me or the girls. I know you'll find that hard to believe, but it's true. I'm sorry, Adam, I know you love him so much and I don't want to ruin your memory of him. He was wonderful to you kids and I loved him for it, because you and Jed hurt so badly when Dad left. But he didn't just want to help out or fill the gap that Dad left, he seemed compelled to be adored. Try and understand; his heart was good but at times he messed up; he wasn't there for me or the girls. Yes, he drove us to the hospital when Kelly cut her leg, but he was too concerned with being your hero to stay with Kelly and me when we needed him. It's not your fault...it's nobody's fault.

He was a good man. I think that he was desperate to be different from his parents, especially his own father who didn't spend any time with him. He seemed to be so desperate to make it right for you boys that he forgot about me and the girls. It's not his fault...it's nobody's fault, it's just the way it was.

It's hard to cope with him gone...I miss him—you get used to someone you live with even if it isn't right—but I don't miss the arguments we had. Things weren't right, Adam. I don't know if you're old enough to understand all this, but I feel that I have to tell you how it really was, because I attacked you and blamed you for everything when it wasn't true...none of it was your fault. My children would have been living without their father anyway, for I was about to leave him. It wasn't right between us. I felt so bad when he died that I wanted to dump my feelings on someone else, and that someone was you. I'm so sorry.

Adam, I'm sorry I haven't visited you; it's because I feel ashamed...but I will if you want me to.

Love always,

Nancy x x x

I feel sick. I'm not sure what to feel. She's bad-mouthing my Tom, my hero, but she's also telling me that none of it was my fault. I feel crushed by her honesty.

"Hey," Saul says, suddenly appearing in front of me, "what's the matter? What's going on?"

He's so on the ball. He seems to figure out anything and everything. He can see that something's wrong just by looking at my face.

"My sister sent me a letter...it's pretty heavy," I say, and I shrug because I don't know what else to say, or what to think. No one in my family has ever been that honest. I hand the letter to him.

He raises an eyebrow as he reads. "That's pretty honest," he says. "How do you feel about it?"

"Part of me wants to punch her on the nose for saying ugly things about Tom, but then again she's apologizing for attacking me and blaming me for his death."

Chelsea joins us, brushing sand from her clothes. "What's the matter?" she asks.

I hand her the letter to read.

"It must have taken some courage to write that," she says. "She's telling you that it's not your fault that Tom died. I mean, *we* all know that, even if *you* won't accept it, but surely hearing it from her will help you to see that his death wasn't your fault."

Saul nods. "Do you think she's right when she says that he wasn't there for her and the kids?"

I don't want to answer him because I don't want to think thoughts that may mess up my memory of Tom, but Saul and Chelsea look at me demanding an answer. Whether I like it or not, an image flashes into my mind.

"I remember feeling awkward on the day he died because Nancy was at our house babysitting the boys along with her kids, too...that's a lot to cope with... the boys can be wild. We were going out to get my girlfriend's birthday cake, and Nancy asked him not to be too long. Tom was mean about her in the car, saying that she was a nag. I blew it off at the time because I guess she can be, but even though she'd asked him to hurry back, he deliberately stayed out all day...he took me bowling. I didn't say anything because I liked being with him and we had a good time, but I was embarrassed when we got back because Nancy went crazy."

"What did he do?"

"Blew her off, had a beer and watched the game,"
I say, hating the direction my thoughts are heading.
"He rolled his eyes when she was crying and said,
'See what I mean?'"

Chelsea looks solemn. "Y'know, Adam, I'd be
mad if I'd been left with all those kids all day and
my husband had deliberately stayed out when he
knew I needed help."

I look at her and she nods.

"No, really, I would be seething. I think I'd be
hurt, too, that my man didn't care about me enough
to help me or to put me first."

"He sounds a bit selfish and irresponsible," Saul
says.

"DON'T," I shout, unable to hear ugly things being
said about my hero.

Chelsea puts her hand on my arm. "We're not
being mean, Adam, we're just trying to help you understand. Sometimes things aren't how they seem. It
sounds to me as if things really weren't okay between
Nancy and Tom."

She falls silent and I stare at the sea, my mind
racing. Did he like being a hero, to be adored by us
boys? It's true that he'd do anything for us and spent
most of his time with us rather than with Nancy and
the girls. He liked doing fun things—he was almost
like a kid himself sometimes—but did that make him
selfish and irresponsible? I don't know what it's like
to be a man or a husband with responsibilities, but I

do know what it's like to be responsible for the boys when I baby-sit them. I know that I would put them first...well, I do. I'd far rather stay in bed than have to make pancakes to keep them amused, but I'd feel bad if I didn't put their needs before my own. I guess that means that I'm a responsible person. So what does it make Tom if he didn't put Nancy and the girls first? As much as I hate it, I think Saul might be right about Tom being selfish and irresponsible, even though he was wonderful to Jed and me. Did he like being adored and hero-worshipped by us? I expect he did, I mean, who wouldn't. I love having Kelly adore me.

I'm not a husband or a father, so I don't really know what that feels like, but I don't believe that I could turn my back on my own kids and my responsibilities even if it was more fun being around other kids.

My head is spinning badly and I feel a bit sick. Why is growing up so hard? Everything seems so complicated.

"C'mon," Chelsea says, giving me a hug. "Let's go in."

It's a long evening and my mind wanders as we watch movies and some of the kids goof off. Even though we have lasagna for dinner, my favorite, I don't have any appetite.

"Are you okay?" Chelsea asks, as I head off to bed early.

"Yeah, I'm fine, I've just got a lot on my mind, that's all. I'll see you tomorrow."

I stand under my shower and let the hot jets of water bombard me, and it feels good but does nothing to get rid of the heaviness in my heart. I turn off the light and get into bed, wanting the day to end. There's a storm outside and I pull the covers up over my head, yet the lightning illuminates the room and I toss and turn, listening to the thunder booming outside. It seems that my efforts to be rid of this day are wasted because I'm wide awake. My head is buzzing and full of thoughts that battle with each other, determined to be heard.

I feel irritated with Nancy for putting thoughts into my head that won't go away now that they're there, and they won't allow me to think as I did before reading her letter. Now that I've remembered how Tom was towards Nancy on the day he died, other memories come flooding into my mind, and no matter how hard I try to get rid of them, I can't.

Jed and I adored him for taking us to a game that we'd been dying to see, and the fact that our team won overshadowed the birth of the twins. I feel a bit sick as it dawns on me that Tom had chosen to take us to the game rather than be there for the birth of his babies. I'd never thought about it before, but now it occurs to me that he took us to a theme park on the day Kelly was born, too. No matter how I try and make excuses for him, I can't ignore the nagging doubt that Nancy is right; he was selfish and irresponsible.

I feel devastated and tears roll down my face. I can't bear thinking negative thoughts about the one person I love with all my heart, but there seems to be no place to hide from the truth anymore.

I don't know how long it takes me to get to sleep; it's long after the storm has past.

I feel half-dead when I wake up in the morning and my eyes are puffy. I hope no one notices, but they do.

We're sitting in the Group Room and Miss Tina says, "Adam, there's something about you that's different. Would you like to say how you're feeling this morning?"

No, actually I wouldn't but I can't say that, and not knowing what to say, I humiliate myself by instantly bursting into tears. I feel foolish and angry with myself. Everyone is staring at me, and so I feel compelled to speak although my instinct is to run, yet again I can't because of my broken leg. Right this minute I think my heart is more broken than my leg is.

"I had a letter from my sister yesterday, and it's messed my head up," I say, trying to gain control of myself. I'm aware that Chelsea is smiling at me and the knowing look on her face gives me some comfort.

"In what way?" Miss Tina asks, scanning the room,

taking in the look on Chelsea's face. She doesn't miss anything...there's no hiding place with her.

I cough and clear my throat. "She told me some things about my brother-in-law that I didn't want to hear, and didn't want to believe...he's always been my hero. I can't bear to think badly of him."

The silence in the room is deafening to me, and Miss Tina slices through it.

"And do you believe these things?" she asks.

I don't want to respond, for to do so will somehow make it real for me, and I don't think I'm ready to face the truth, but once again the kids are all staring at me and so I feel obliged to answer.

"Yes, I hate it but I think the things Nancy said are true." I can feel despair wash through me and I look straight into Miss Tina's face, praying that she can throw me a lifeline, for I sure as hell need one.

"Of all the things she said, what made you think badly of him?"

"She said that he was selfish and the only thing that really mattered to him was to be a hero to me and my brothers. She said that he neglected her and their three babies..." I swallow hard, "...and I know that's true. But I can't get it out of my head how good he was to me...I loved him for it. She said that he'd try to take the place of my dad."

"Do you think that's true?" she asks.

I hate what's happening to me, for a huge wave of misery swamps me as memories of my dad leaving drown me. An awful sob escapes me and I long to throw up.

I don't know how many minutes pass before I'm able to lift my head from my hands and quiet my breathing.

"Do you think that Tom tried to take the place of your father?" Miss Tina asks again.

I nod. "Yes, I think so…"

Every part of me hurts.

"But why did he have to neglect his own family in order to be there for us? It makes me feel awful."

"His behavior is not your responsibility, though," she says. "He had his own reasons for wanting to step in and be a father to you, and also his own reasons for failing his family. None of it is your responsibility."

I glance around; Saul and Chelsea are nodding.

Miss Tina has a gentle look on her face and says, "I think you should be thankful for what Tom gave you. You have no reason to feel any guilt about having benefited from the care he wanted to give you. It's not your fault that your father left you. Perhaps any anger you feel should be directed at him, not anyone else. Tom, for whatever his reasons were, wanted to be there for you and your brothers…he gave you something precious, be thankful. It's okay to realize that he wasn't perfect, that he made mistakes, and it's okay to love him even though he hurt his family."

I can feel a solitary tear slide down my face as I

battle with my love for him while recognizing that he wasn't the perfect person I thought he was. I don't even have the energy to hate my father for leaving us, but if he hadn't left perhaps I wouldn't have idolized Tom, and Tom wouldn't have felt the need to be a hero for me and Jed, and then perhaps he'd have been a better husband and father. But I'm playing the "what if" game again. I try to block out my thoughts as soon as I realize what I'm doing.

I look up and Chelsea and Saul are smiling at me, and I give them a watery smile back.

"I don't want to mess up my memories of him," I say, looking at Miss Tina. "I don't want my Wisteria flowers on my dead tree to be shriveled and horrible...I don't want to have horrible memories of him."

Miss Tina rescues me. "Adam, no human being is perfect. Don't feel badly towards Tom because you now realize that he wasn't perfect. Treasure your memories of him and the times you had with him. Let them be the Wisteria blooms on Tom's withered tree; let them keep him alive for you."

I smile at her and suddenly feel peaceful. Yes, that's what I'll do, remember all the fun times we had. It's not my responsibility to feel bad about the relationship he had with Nancy or the problems they had.

She lets us go for lunch and tells us to look at the lilac flowers growing over a fence on the far side of the playground. "That's Wisteria," she says.

After we've eaten we hang out on the playground and Chelsea says, "Wow, look at that," nodding towards the fence that's loaded with Wisteria, "it really is beautiful, isn't it? I can picture how a withered tree would seem as if it had come back to life."

She's right, it is beautiful. I'm going to keep my good memories of Tom and see them as the lilac lantern-shaped flowers that are very much alive, which cover something that isn't.

It's time to go back inside. Miss Tina's already in the Group Room.

"Okay, let's back up a bit. I want to ask you a question, Adam."

I sit up straight, wondering what she's going to ask me.

She looks at me, and says, "What else did your sister say in her letter?"

"Shall I read it out loud?" I ask. I don't mind, after all, I've already shown it to Saul, R.J. and Chelsea.

"If you feel comfortable doing so."

I read it.

Miss Tina says, "How does it make you feel to know that your sister doesn't blame you for your brother-in-law's death?"

I sit in silence trying to gather my thoughts; how do I feel knowing that Nancy doesn't blame me? I'm not sure.

"I don't know," I say. "I'm relieved that she's not going to attack me again, but I still feel guilty and I don't know how to make it go away. I can think through all the things she's said, and you've said," I glance around, "that all of you have said, and I understand them with my brain, but my heart just won't believe them. I still feel guilty."

"What do you think guilt is?" Miss Tina asks, looking around the room at everyone. I'm glad she's not just looking at me because I don't know how to answer her.

"It's what you feel when you've done something wrong," a kid says.

"Not always," Chelsea all but snaps at him. "It could be when you feel bad about something that's happened when you *believe* that it might be your fault; it doesn't mean to say that it *is* your fault. Some people do things wrong and don't care—they don't feel guilt—and other people feel guilt when they haven't done anything wrong."

"Well, you're both right," Miss Tina says. "It's a feeling inside you that happens when you've done something wrong or believe that you've done something wrong. Where does guilt come from?"

No one answers, not even Chelsea, who seems to know so much.

"Human beings aren't born with a conscience; they have to learn about right and wrong, and about how doing wrong towards others makes them feel bad. They also have to care about other people to develop a conscience. Chelsea's right, if someone doesn't care about other people, then they won't care if they do wrong things towards them, and so they won't feel guilt. Feeling guilt shows that you have a healthy conscience and that your parents have brought you up to care about others and taught you to try not to hurt other people; that's good. Feeling guilty when you've hurt someone is healthy because it causes you to try and make amends, to try and make things better by apologizing and learning from the experience. But what happens when guilt becomes unhealthy?"

My stomach flips, as I just know she's going to turn towards me. And she does.

"Adam, you are eaten up with guilt, aren't you? Although you've heard everything everybody's said to you, and you've read your sister's letter which tells you that you aren't to blame for Tom's death in any way, you're still eaten up with guilt. Am I right?"

I glance around the room. No one's going to help me answer her question—there's only her and me—with the truth hovering in the space between us.

"Yes," I mumble.

I don't need to repeat myself, as the room is so quiet that everyone can hear me.

"Did you murder your brother-in-law?"

"No!"

"Did you force him to drive dangerously?"

"No, but he knew I was anxious because we were late."

She seems determined to pin me down.

"Okay, you were late, but did you force him to drive dangerously?"

"No!" I say, with irritation coursing through me.

"Did you force him to spend more time with you than with his wife and girls?"

"NO!" I shout, feeling suddenly hateful towards Miss Tina.

Her voice changes, becoming soft, leaving my anger echoing in the silence.

"People make their own choices, Adam. Every one of us is responsible for the choices we make, even if they turn out badly. It's a tough lesson, but it's one of the most important things you'll ever learn. Own what belongs to you, take responsibility for the things you do wrong, and yes, feel guilty because you need to do something right to make amends to those you hurt. But if it's not your responsibility when something goes wrong, then you have no reason to feel guilty.

Some kids are shifting in their seats, but I'm barely aware of them. I feel nailed to the floor by Miss Tina's words.

"You *know* these things, Adam, you're a smart boy. You must see that you have no reason to feel guilty about Tom's death. And yet I see guilt written all over you...your face is full of it. What have you done wrong, or *believe* that you've done wrong, that causes you to feel such guilt?"

My head begins to spin so badly that I don't know what to do. I don't know how to answer...the silence in the room is deafening. I feel incredibly sick and want to vomit; my thoughts and feelings seem like a jumbled mess churning in my stomach. Images flash into my head, and not one of them is of Tom. They're of Becky and, to my horror, the old prostitute I visited time and time again. My face flushes and burns as shame floods through me.

I don't know how to answer so that I won't feel stripped naked in front of all these kids, but I know I've got to say something to silence their staring.

"I blamed my girlfriend. I told her that Tom died because of her stupid birthday party...I ripped up all her photos...I hurt her and I wanted to...I wanted her to hurt as much as I was hurting. I finished with her and then..."

My voice becomes a whisper and I stare at the floor.

"...And then I started sleeping with a prostitute, and I just couldn't stop myself." I hang my head in my hands, trying to hide my shame.

"I can't go back to Becky now, even if I wanted to. I feel so dirty and ashamed of myself."

I feel mortified, expecting Miss Tina to frown with disappointment in me, and the kids to jeer, but nothing happens; there's absolute silence in the room. I gradually look up, and as I battle to shake the revolting images out of my mind, I see acceptance on Miss Tina's face.

She breaks the silence and throws me a lifeline.

"Sometimes when people are grieving and feel so bad that they wish they were dead, they can be desperate for something or someone to remind them that they're alive. Some people seek an adrenaline rush and do crazy things that excite them, and other people do things that force the body to feel, to feel *anything*.

"Remember everything I taught you about 'dis-association'; remember Ken's balloons. The human brain is destined to be healthy, and when a person is gripped in the agony of grief, where he longs to feel absolutely nothing, the brain will do almost anything to force that person to feel something... anything."

Miss Tina looks at me and holds me in her gaze. "Adam, don't you realize that by visiting a prostitute you coped in the only way you knew how at the time? She enabled you to feel something...she offered you a bridge between life and oblivion. Do not feel bad, do not feel guilt for what you felt you had to do in order to stay alive when your grief was so bad that all you wanted to do was die."

Something breaks inside me and I begin to sob... the noise seems to be coming from far away.

R.J. looks at me with admiration on his face.

"I think your honesty is awesome," he says, and one by one the kids agree with him.

"Can I give you a hug?" Chelsea says, darting out of her chair and throwing her arms around me. "You're so wonderful," she whispers before going back to her chair.

Miss Tina smiles at me. I feel reassured that these kids aren't going to reject or judge me, and I feel calmed and accepted. My tears have gone, and I suddenly feel free of the shame and guilt that has gripped me since Tom died.

Miss Tina waits until everyone gets quiet and then speaks.

"Adam, do not feel guilty about what you did to help you feel alive when you were swamped with grief." She turns and faces us all. "People often engage in reckless behavior when they're grieving, and the reason for such behavior is to force the body to feel *something* when grief forces their feelings to 'shut down' because it can't stand the pain. It's like a war between feeling and not feeling. Understand why you behave the way you did, and then let it go. Learn from it, okay?"

I nod, feeling a weird sense of calm come over me.

"I've felt so bad about it," I confess. "I feel so dirty, and I've been scared that I might have caught something from her."

"Tell me you used a condom," R.J. says.

"Of course."

Miss Tina nods. "I don't need to tell you all that if you must have sex, for heaven sake use a condom."

Although she suddenly sounds stern, I don't feel that she's lecturing us.

"Listen, Adam, it's unlikely that you'll have caught anything from her as you used a condom, but to make sure, I'll arrange for you to see the doctor, okay?"

I nod, feeling embarrassed but glad that somebody finally knows and can make all the worry and shame go away.

Chapter Eleven

Miss Tina lets us go, and after grabbing a soda we head outside. I can't believe how light I feel. It's as if someone has relieved me of a huge, ugly growth around my neck that weighed me down and threatened to suffocate me. I still feel ashamed, although now that it's out in the open, my shame feels more like embarrassment. I feel a bit sheepish in front of the other kids and don't really know what to say. I don't have to worry, though, because they just go about their business and all but ignore me, like it doesn't matter and is no big deal to them.

Saul holds my soda while I lower myself down onto the grass, and then he flops down beside me.

"Hey, man, tell me," he says, quietly, "what's it like having sex with a prostitute?"

I'm embarrassed, but he says, "No, really, I want to know."

"It's disgusting," I say, shuddering. "Okay, your body feels good for a split second, but then your brain kicks in and you feel disgusted...well, I did."

I look out to sea, watching the waves gently roll up the sand. I think I understand everything Miss Tina said. I understand why I did it, and why I kept on doing it, but that doesn't change the way I feel right now. I wanted my first time to be with Becky, not with some woman older than my mother. There's a lump in my throat as I feel a sense of loss that has nothing to do with losing Tom.

A fresh wave of love for Becky comes over me that is quickly swamped by shame at the way I treated her. Her dad said that he would have punched me for behaving the way I did towards her, had I not been grieving...I feel worse.

"What?" I say, having totally missed what Saul was saying.

"I said, was it your first time?"

"Yeah, it was, and that's what makes it hard to deal with. Becky and I were in love, big time, and we'd decided to wait. I wanted my first time to be with her. I know it sounds stupid, but that's how it was."

"Hey, it's not stupid. My first time was with this gorgeous girl..."

He rolls over onto his back and howls. He makes me laugh.

"What happened? Are you still with her?"

He rolls back over onto his side and looks straight into my face, suddenly serious.

"Yeah, I am. Does that surprise you? She's amazing, and besides that, it's a jungle out there. I don't want to sleep around, if you know what I mean..." he nudges me, "because how can you tell who's clean and who isn't? There are so many diseases out there, and I'm not catching one, oh no, not me."

"Do you love her?"

He's quiet for a moment and then says, "Yeah, I guess I do. She's stuck by me through everything, and that says a lot."

We become quiet, lost in our own thoughts. Suddenly I feel more alone than I've ever felt, and there's a pang in my heart that consumes me.

R.J. flops down on the grass next to us.

"What're you guys talking about?"

Saul jolts me back to the patch of grass I'm sitting on.

"We're talking about having sex."

I flinch. I don't want to keep going over my shame at having sex with a prostitute.

"What about it?" he asks.

"I asked Adam what it was like having sex with a prostitute."

"And..." R.J. asks, looking at me for an answer.

"I told him it was bad, and I wish it'd been with my girlfriend who I loved, and Saul said that his first time was with a girl he was crazy about."

"What about you?" Saul asks him. "Who was your first?"

"Some whore at school; it was no big deal. Everyone's had her," he shrugs. "It was no big deal."

"But don't you feel bad that it wasn't special?" Saul asks. "Okay, so I've never had sex with someone that I don't care about, so I guess it's hard to make a comparison, but sleeping with my girl was awesome because I adored her."

R.J. looks blank. "I guess I don't know what you're talking about; it was there on offer and I took it. It felt good at the time, but it meant nothing."

I know what he means and I hate it. I want what Saul's got, not something that means nothing. I want to share that amazing sexual feeling that takes over your whole body with someone I love, not with someone who doesn't care about me, or who only wants my money. I look at R.J.; I can't think poorly of him because he's being honest, and that makes me feel respect for him. But I hate what he's saying because I know that I've behaved as he has. I want what Saul's got. I had no idea that having sex was so complicated, but it is, and I feel that I've messed up big time.

"Help me up," I say, urgently.

Saul yanks me up and I limp off through the playground towards the doors. I have to tell Becky I'm sorry. I don't know how to do it, but I'm going to try.

As I reach the reception area where the phones are, I suddenly feel a bit stupid. She won't speak to me, not after the awful things I said to her. I don't know what to do, so I hover by the phone, messing around with the change in my pocket as if I'm looking for a quarter. I feel nervous and let another kid use the phone before me, but when he finishes, I'm left to make a decision that I'm not ready for. I chicken out and call Mom. I ask her to call Becky to tell her I'm sorry for the way I acted. I can hear in Mom's voice that she's pleased. I hang up feeling triumphant yet frustrated. Suddenly this seems to be the most important thing in my life, and I've left it to my mom to fix.

If I weren't on crutches, I'd pace up and down, but I can't, so I go back outside and join Saul and R.J. Chelsea's there as well.

"You called her, didn't you?" Saul asks, and I want to lie, feeling embarrassed that I couldn't face my girlfriend, after the way I'd treated her, and had to get my mom to do it for me.

"No, I didn't," I say, which is technically not a lie. "I called my mom."

They mess around and don't question me, for which I'm grateful, and as I sit there watching the kids goofing off on the sand, it occurs to me that they've given me something precious. They heard my story, witnessed my shame, and yet they've accepted me as one of them. I suddenly feel overwhelmed, and as I look around at Saul, R.J. and Chelsea, it seems as if the sound has been turned off while I'm watching a movie. I smile to myself. I love this place and I love these kids.

"You seen her latest video? She's hot," R.J. says.

"What? Who?"

"Oh, never mind," he says, grinning at me. "Go back to sleep."

We have the rest of the day off, to "rest and grow," I guess, and I need to do both.

I tell them that I've got stuff to do, and Saul helps me up. They go down onto the beach with the rest of the kids as I go back inside. I don't feel jealous anymore, as there's something I have to do.

I call Mom again, and she tells me that Becky wasn't in. I feel frustrated, as I want to set things right this very minute. I know, I'll write her a letter. That's what Nancy did, so that's what I'll do. I limp off to the classroom and find a piece of paper.

At first I don't know what to say or where to begin, but when I think about the pain on her face when I blamed her for Tom's death, I know exactly where to start. When I look up at the clock, it's two hours later, and there are several scrunched up balls of paper on the floor where I've started and messed up. But finally I've got a letter in front of me that I'm sort of satisfied with. It says:

Dear Becky,
I doubt that you will ever be able to forgive me for the way I treated you after Tom died. I can't ask

you to forgive me, for it's too much to hope for, but I do hope that you'll try and understand instead.

I blamed myself for Tom's death because I feel that I put pressure on him to get me to your house on time on your birthday. He drove too fast, and I begged him to slow down, but he wouldn't.

When I realized he was dead, it hurt so much, and I couldn't cope with the pain. So I tried to dump it onto someone else, and the only person I could do that to was someone close to me, and that was you. I'm so sorry.

I think I was a bit crazy at the time and wasn't thinking straight. I felt that the sight of you forced me to blame myself all over again for Tom's death, and I couldn't cope with it, so I dumped on you the blame I felt. I know it's sick. I didn't intend to hurt you. I was just hurting so badly that I wanted to die and make the pain go away. I felt cheated that I had lived and he hadn't. I know that sounds crazy, but that's how I felt. Every time I saw Nancy and the girls, I wanted to die; I felt that I'd robbed the girls of their father, and the guilt was unbearable.

I can barely remember the things I said to you, but I do remember what your father said to me. I saw disappointment and anger in his face, and God forgive me, because I think your father's great, but I didn't care. I wanted him to hit me, to smash me into oblivion. I wanted to die.

But since I've been at Beach Haven, I've learned

so much. I've learned to accept the things that are my responsibility and to ignore the things that have nothing to do with me. I've also learned about grief and that much of my behavior was normal, which makes me feel a lot better. But the one thing that still makes me feel bad is the way I treated you, even though I now understand why I behaved as I did.

I loved you so much, you meant everything to me, and I was desperate to please you and make your birthday special. Tom and I had planned it for weeks, along with your parents, and we had it down to the last second. When it all went wrong, I couldn't cope.

I wanted your birthday to be so special, and when I ask myself why, I realize that it's because my birthdays meant nothing in my family and it hurt, so I wanted yours to mean something. It wasn't your fault that I was determined to make your birthday great; it was what I wanted...which would make it right for me. Then everything went wrong and, because I couldn't cope with it, I blamed you. I know I hurt you, and I'm so sorry. I don't expect you to forgive me. I just want you to understand why I behaved that way—and your Dad's right; I do need a punch on the nose.

I'd give anything to suffer the pain of a broken nose rather than the pain of knowing that I hurt you when you didn't deserve any of it. There's nothing I can do other than to say I'm sorry and hope you

understand that I was out of my mind with grief and
guilt.

   Love,

   Adam

   I don't put kisses because I think I've been "real" enough, and if she kicks me to the curb, as I think she will, it'll lessen my humiliation. Yeah, right, I don't think so; nothing can lessen the humiliation and emptiness I feel at having lost the one person who has always been there for me. I feel sad and ashamed of myself. I want to cry.

   I sit staring at the letter, thinking about all the things I've learned since coming to Beach Haven and how much I've changed.

   Why is it that we hurt those who love us the most? I think it's because we can. I hate the thoughts that pop into my head. I remember wanting to be just like Tom—to be smooth and have the power he had over Nancy. He would just blow her off when she got mad at him, and he always seemed to be able to get his own way, but the thought sickens me now. I don't want to be like that. I want to be "real" and to let my girlfriend know that I'm real. I don't want to be like Tom, able to hurt someone because he could. I don't want to be like R.J. either—someone who only wants sex without caring about the girl he uses.

   I like R.J. He makes me laugh, but I don't like where he's coming from. He forces me to face myself. I've done what he has, used someone for sex, and I hate how I feel about myself and what I did. I wonder what he's seen and heard that makes it okay for him to have sex with someone he doesn't care about. Although I like him, I don't want to be the same as him, or think the same way he does. I have my own ideas, my own thoughts about being in a relationship and having sex. I don't care if that makes me different from other kids my age; I just want to be me and do the right thing.

I move towards the window. The sun's setting, slipping down towards the sea. There's something wonderful about watching the sun set over the sea; everything sparkles.

I take the letter to the lady in reception and she puts it in the mail; now all I have to do is wait.

"Oh, there you are," Saul says, coming around the corner. "Where've you been?"

I trust Saul. He knows so much but, more importantly, he respects his girlfriend, so I know he'll understand how I'm feeling.

"I've been writing a letter to Becky to apologize for the way I treated her. I don't suppose it'll do any good, but it needed to be said anyway."

He looks at me and knows that I haven't said what I'm feeling.

"I hope you can sort it out. It hurts, doesn't it? I know, I've been there. I lost a girlfriend once after I messed up big time."

I don't know what to say because I feel like crying. I feel empty, but I have to be strong. I've messed up big time and now I have to accept the consequences of my behavior. I hurt Becky so much that I'm certain she won't want anything to do with me ever again.

"C'mon, let's go and join the others," he says, looking me straight in the eye and rescuing me from the pit I'm about to fall into. I hobble after him and hear the kids laughing and messing around.

"Hey, Adam, where've you been? We've got pizza; you want some? We're just going to watch a movie. I saved you a seat," Chelsea calls out.

Nancy says, "There's a seat here, too."

Saul bumps into me on purpose and whispers in my ear. "Hey man, they're falling over you..." and he shakes his head as he flops down on a sofa.

I feel a bit irritated; I don't want girls falling over me. I only want Becky. Okay, so I know some of the girls here like me. So what? I like them, but I'm not interested in any of them in that way, not even Chelsea, who's awesome.

I find myself a chair and throw my crutches on the floor, preparing to stick my leg out and lower myself back, when the reception lady appears at the door.

"Hey, Adam, you've got a visitor."

I'm poised in mid-air, my body halfway between standing and sitting and my mind praying that my visitor is Becky. Yet I know that I've only just finished writing to her, so it can't be her.

Chelsea looks up, then hands me my crutches and says, "See you later."

I follow the reception lady back up the hall. I can't go as fast as she can, but she waits for me, holding the visitor's room door open.

"There you are," she says, and leaves.

I stand in the doorway. An involuntary shiver trickles down my spine; Nancy stands when she sees me.

"Adam..."

She moves towards me and tears start rolling down her face.

"Oh, Adam, are you all right?"

She's flustered and nervous, I guess. I'm nervous, too, but as she throws her arms around me, I feel accepted and my fears melt away. I was scared that I would see blame on her face, but there's none. She almost pulls me over and then giggles as she tries to hold me up.

"Here, come and sit down."

I limp into the room, letting my crutches fall to the floor, and I lower myself gently into a chair opposite her.

"Oh, Adam, Mom told me that you read my letter. Thank you. I feel so bad. None of this was your fault. I feel so awful for attacking you...I was crazy that night and I lashed out. I'm so sorry, babe, can you forgive me?" She's talking too fast and I know she's nervous. I want to reassure her.

"There's nothing to forgive, okay? You did what I did to Becky, and believe me, I feel awful, too. I guess when something bad happens and we feel awful, we try to push it onto someone else."

She wipes her nose and nods.

"Have you heard from Becky?" she asks.

"Nope, I've written to her and we'll see what she says. I don't expect her to forgive me, though. I was awful to her."

"No more awful than I was to you. Do you forgive me?"

I want her to stop. There's nothing to forgive, but she seems to want something from me and carries on.

"Do you? Do you forgive me for the way I treated you? None of this was your fault. Tom was headstrong; he always did what he wanted to do, and nothing I said made any difference. I'm not badmouthing him, not at all, I loved him in my own way and I think he loved me, too. But we just didn't have what it takes to stay together. We were about to split up when he died. Things were about to change, but it just happened sooner than I expected, and in a different way. None of it was your fault."

"I know," I say, suddenly feeling very wise. I've learned so much at Beach Haven, where there's no place to hide anything or to be fake. I've examined all my feelings and owned what's mine, so I can sit here and listen to Nancy struggling with the truth and know where I stand, what is my responsibility and what isn't.

"How're the girls?" I ask, breaking an awkward silence when she finishes apologizing over and over. "Mom brought Kelly to see me the other day. She was funny; she showed me her leg."

"They're fine. Kelly's stopped asking when Tom's going to come home...in fact the only person she asks about is you. She adores you, Adam, do you know that?"

I swallow hard, thinking of the smile on her face and the acceptance she gives me, no matter who I am or what I've done.

"Yeah, I love her, too."

"She's dying for you to come home. D'you know when you're going to be able to come home? We all miss you, especially the boys. Well, actually it isn't only the boys that long for you to come home, it's Mom, too, and Jed. There's a big hole in our family when you're not there," she says.

"Yeah, and Sherrie misses me, does she?" I say sarcastically.

Nancy's face falters for a moment. "Well, not exactly, but you know her, so don't let it bother you. Everyone in our family loves you, and we want you home. Don't let her get to you, it's just not worth it." She seems to drift off. "I've had to endure it all my life and, although it makes me feel awful, I've tried really hard to please her so that she'd be nice to you boys. It hasn't been easy, and Mom was no help. She just gave in to her to keep her quiet, but since Tom died Mom seems to be stronger. They had a big fight the other day and Mom told her that she wasn't welcome at the house until she got her act together." She grins at me. "It was awesome...you should have seen Sherrie's face."

I grin; I'd give anything to have been there.

"Anyway, I think things will be easier for you boys now."

She gives me a hug as she leaves and tells me she loves me.

• • • •

The days go by and, as each one passes without Becky calling, I struggle with an overwhelming feeling of emptiness and sadness. I knew it was too much to expect her to forgive me. I guess this is where I really grow up and accept the consequences of my actions. I don't feel ready. Everyone keeps asking me what's wrong and I say, "Nothing," but of course Saul and Chelsea don't believe me.

"She'll come around," he says, but I'm not re-assured. He can't know for sure, and as the days pass, I feel more hopeless and resigned to the fact that I screwed up so badly that nothing can put it right. It's a horrible feeling.

Saul and R.J. try to cheer me up by turning on the radio and singing along. They take turns in telling each other that they can't sing. I'd laugh if I weren't so down. Chelsea sits close to me and rubs my arm.

"Hey, Adam, come on, it'll be okay."

I shrug, feeling so depressed that I don't know what to do. I've learned so much about grieving, about being in touch with my feelings and coping with them, but my feelings all come flooding back like a tidal wave, drowning me in misery. At times when I'm alone, I almost feel as bad as I did on the day Tom died. Why does all this hurt so much?

We're sitting in group one morning and Miss Tina looks at me. "Adam, you've seemed very down lately. What's going on?"

I feel so miserable that I don't even want to speak, but of course I have to, since everyone's looking at me.

I shrug. "I don't know. I feel as bad as I did the day Tom died, and I thought that after all the work I've done here to help me understand everything about grief, I'd be able to manage my feelings better." I feel hopeless.

"I wrote a letter to my girlfriend," I say, "to tell her how sorry I am for being so mean and blaming her for Tom's death, and I guess I expected her to get back to me." As I say it, I sound arrogant. Just because I'm ready to apologize, I expect her to be ready to forgive me.

I shrug again. "I guess some things just can't be fixed." I feel sick.

There's something on Miss Tina's face that looks like a frown, sorrow and pity, and she shrugs, too.

"Maybe so. I don't know. Just give her time. She needs time to rest and grow, too—everyone does—and sometimes it takes people different amounts of time to come to terms with things. Don't lose faith, Adam. You did the right thing. You owned your behavior and you apologized for hurting her; whether she accepts your apology is going to come down to the type of person she is. She may feel so hurt that nothing you say will make any difference, and you are going to have to accept that."

I know she sees my face drop.

"I know that's hard, but that's how it is. You've been honest and you can't do any more than that. What do you feel for her?" she asks.

I can feel tears pricking my eyes and instantly feel angry with myself, but I can't stop them rolling down my face.

"I love her...I always have. We've been together for two years. I can't believe that I treated her so badly," I shake my head. How could I have been so stupid? I haven't only lost Tom; I've lost the girl I'm crazy about. I feel as much grief over losing Becky as I do about losing Tom, and that makes no sense to me, but that's how it is.

Miss Tina sits up in her chair. "Y'know, you don't only feel grief when you lose someone through death; you can experience it when you feel any sense of loss. Adam's going through the grieving process, as he believes that his relationship with Becky is beyond repair. That's a normal feeling," she says.

"Yeah, but I don't get it," I say, suddenly animated and angry. "I was coming to terms with Tom's death, but now I feel as bad as I did at the beginning. I feel like I haven't...*grown*...at all." I know I sound sarcastic, but I can't help it. I feel as bad as I did the day Tom died, so I can't possibly have grown at all.

"Listen, all of you, the grieving process is like a journey. It's hard and painful, but it's a journey where the destination is never in doubt. You *will* make it and you *will* get there, safe and sound. You will get through this and find yourself in a place where you can smile at your memories of the one you've lost. In many ways it's easier to lose someone through death, for you haven't really lost them. Those we love live in our hearts and in our memories, and we can feel the love we shared just by thinking about them. The grief we feel when we lose someone through the breakup of a relationship is often harder because we have to accept that they *chose* to leave us, whereas those we lose through death didn't."

I wipe my nose on my sleeve, feeling terrible.

"Sometimes we just have to accept that the person has gone and that our lives will go on without them in it. It's hard, I know, but you have to make a leap of faith and believe that life is working out as it should, and in the future you will look back on this and reflect upon the 'what if' game.

"Y'know, when I look back on my life, at some of the times when I felt as if my world was falling apart, at those times the direction of my life changed and with it came a whole new world, one with hope. When I look back now, I know that if some things hadn't happened, I wouldn't be with you all now."

She smiles at us. "I look back and think, 'Wow, if everything had turned out as I was desperate for it to at that time, then everything about my life would have taken a different path and I wouldn't have met the people I now know, nor would I be here.' So even though I suffered pain when things didn't turn out the way I wanted them to, I've grown, and my life is working out in the way that it should."

No one speaks, and she becomes silent, lost in her memories.

Is this what is supposed to happen in my life? Were Becky and I destined to split up? I can't answer my own question, and suddenly I don't feel the need to. Maybe this is like the checkers game that Miss Cassie told us about—different moves going in different directions but all heading towards an ending that's inevitable.

I look at the floor, my tears gone. I feel my jaw tighten and some strength flow through me. Will I look back on this moment and think in the future, when I'm a man, that although I hurt so badly right now, this was a fork in the road of my life? Will I? I don't know. But whatever the future brings, Miss Tina's words throw me a lifeline and I grab it.

"Grief is a journey, one where you'll be weary and in pain, but one where you can still enjoy the view. You can still laugh and have fun even though you mourn the one you've lost. It's a journey where you think you've almost cracked it, you're almost at your destination. But then you're dashed into despair, and you believe that you're back at square one. But all these things are part of the journey; and you *will* arrive at the destination—acceptance.

"What you need to do is to manage your grief. One way is to make a contract with yourself to spend just one hour a day to grieve physically, to cry. When you've done that, put all your feelings of grief away until the next time you allow yourself to visit them. This exercise gives you power over your feelings. It values the grief you feel, yet enables you to learn to control your feelings so that you can still enjoy life while you grieve. Try it."

Miss Tina stands up and opens the double doors out into the playground. "It's a beautiful evening; go outside...rest and grow."

I haul myself up and Saul hands me my crutches. Chelsea goes back into the Group Room, but I follow Saul and R.J. out onto the edge of the playground.

"Are you all right?" Saul asks me.

I nod, feeling different, but okay. He takes my crutches and helps me lower myself down on the outer limits of the playground, before the grass loses itself to the sand. I'm just about to drop myself into Saul and R.J.'s hands when Chelsea calls out.

"No! Not tonight."

She walks over to us carrying trash bags.

"Tonight you're going to cover up so that no sand can get into your cast, and you're going to come with us down onto the beach."

Saul and R.J. leap to their feet and grab me while Chelsea begins to thread the plastic bags over my broken leg, and I flush bright red when she anchors it around my groin.

"Okay! You ready?" they ask, grinning at me.

I put my arms around their shoulders. Chelsea calls Nancy over and they each grab one of my legs. They walk the few yards to the shore and then dump me at the water's edge.

Saul hovers around, picking things up while I lean on R.J. so that I don't fall over.

"Here," Saul says, putting pebbles into my hand. "Throw them as far as you can."

I throw with all my might and the kids cheer. I can smell the salt in the air, and the sound of the waves rushing up the sand fills my ears.

"Cool."

We stand there for ages, skimming stones to see who can get theirs the furthest, and I lose all concept of time. The sunset is awesome. I feel my depression evaporating. I feel peaceful.

While the kids are goofing around, I sit on the sand, my leg protected by the trash bags. The sun slips towards the horizon, destined to disappear. The kids drift away, and I tell them I'm fine. I want to be alone for awhile, with the waves that roll up the sand to keep me company.

Miss Tina's right, the ocean is so peaceful and calming. I throw the last few pebbles into the waves, hoping that they'll skim across the water, and when they do, I smile and let out a triumphant, "Yes!"

"Good shot," someone says, and instantly I freeze.

It's Becky. She stands above me, wringing her hands, which tells me that she's as nervous as I am.

"Becky!" I gasp, my heart hammering in my chest. I can't stand up, and I suddenly feel very vulnerable.

"I got your letter," she says awkwardly.

"Oh, yeah, good, right," I stutter.

There's an awkward silence between us. I don't know what to do, and I'm scared to death that I'm going to mess up the one chance I have to put it right between us.

She drops down beside me, puts her arms around her knees, and stares out to sea. I stare out to sea, too, shielding my eyes from the glare of the sinking sun, but then we both look at each other and start to speak.

"I, um..."

"Did you..."

"Oh, sorry."

"No, you go first." I give her a bleak smile.

"Thanks for writing to me," she says.

She gives me an opening and I grab it. "I'm so sorry, Becky. I know I hurt you badly and you didn't deserve any of it. Can you forgive me?" I ask.

She looks at me, and there are tears glistening in her eyes. "You really hurt me, Adam; you broke my heart."

There's a sinking feeling in my stomach as the flash of hope I felt at seeing her flickers. Is she going to tell me that it's over for good, and that we can't get back together? I feel so sick.

"I know and I'm so sorry." I feel like a man begging for his life before being given a death sentence. "I was crazy with grief and I didn't know how to handle it...I wasn't thinking straight."

I'm babbling and just repeat everything I wrote in the letter, but I don't know what else to say.

"Shhh," she says, "I understand. I was so heartbroken, and then angry, that I never wanted to see you ever again. But thanks to your letter, I think I understand. Yes, of course I forgive you."

My heart soars. "Does that mean we can get back together?" I ask, feeling more confident, but the look on her face dashes my hopes.

"I don't know." She shakes her head. "I really don't know, Adam. I still love you, I've never really stopped, but I don't know if we can go back to how we were. I don't know if it's possible. You've wrecked the trust I had in you, and I don't know how to get it back. I want to, but I just don't know how."

She looks at me and there's no denying that I can see love in her eyes, but I can also see pain and betrayal.

I don't know what to say for I don't have the answers. How do you repair trust that is broken? I decide to be honest; there's nothing else I can do.

"Becky, you mean more to me than anything. I've learned so much being here and it's been really painful. I've learned all about grief and the grieving process." She frowns.

"And I've learned that most of my behavior was a normal reaction to shock and grief. I'm not excusing my behavior," I say quickly. "What I did to you was terrible, and I'd do anything to take it back, but I can't. I just hope that you'll understand why I behaved as I did. I felt like I'd lost my mind."

I get a fleeting urge to tell her about the balloons that represent Ken's brain, but then balloons and Becky are like an open wound to me, so I don't. Besides, I'm in such a panic that I doubt if I'll make any sense.

"I know I've wrecked the trust you had in me,

but can't we start again as two people who've both known pain and who have learned from it?"

She looks at me as the last glimmer from the sinking sun leaves a golden path across the ocean and casts her shadow over my face. A tear rolls down her cheek.

She leans forward and kisses me. "Yes," she cries, and holds me as we cry together until the sun slips away.

She hands me a tissue and we blow our noses noisily and giggle. She nestles next to me, and I stare out to sea. My journey on the checkerboard of life has just taken a different route. Tom's "piece" was taken early in the "game," and I almost lost Becky's "piece."

I smile to myself as I watch the moon replace the sun and cast shadows on the sand around us. She smiles at me with forgiveness in her eyes.

About the Author

Dr. Celia Banting earned her Ph.D. by studying suicide attempts in adolescents and developing a risk assessment tool to identify those young people who may be at risk of attempting suicide. She identified several risk factors which, when combined, could increase the likelihood of an individual attempting suicide. Rather than write "how to" books or text books to help teenagers cope with the risk factors, Dr. Banting has incorporated therapeutic interventions into novels that adolescents will be able to identify with. These novels are designed to increase the adolescents' ability to take care of themselves, should they have minimal support in their families.

Dr. Banting's career has revolved around caring for children in a variety of settings in both the United Kingdom and the United States. She is dedicated to helping troubled children avoid the extreme act of suicide.

WIGHITA PRESS ORDER FORM

Book Title	Price	Qty.	Total

I Only Said I Had No Choice
ISBN 0-9786648-0-9 $14.99   x _____ $_____
Shane learns how to control his anger and make positive life
choices; and he gains understanding about adult co-dependency.

I Only Said "Yes" So That They'd Like Me
ISBN 0-9786648-1-7 $14.99   x _____ $_____
Melody learns how to cope with being bullied by the in-crowd at
school and explores the emotional consequences of casual sex.
She raises her self-esteem and learns what true beauty is.

I Only Said I Couldn't Cope
ISBN 0-9786648-2-5 $14.99   x _____ $_____
Adam learns how to deal with grief and depression. He works
through the grieving process and explores his perceptions of
death and life.

I Only Said I Didn't Want You Because I Was Terrified
ISBN 0-9786648-3-3 $14.99   x _____ $_____
Hannah experiences peer pressure to drink alcohol. She learns
about teenage pregnancy, birth, and caring for a new baby.
Hannah faces the consequences of telling lies and learns how to
repair broken trust.

I Only Said I Was Telling the Truth
ISBN 0-9786648-4-1 $14.99   x _____ $_____
Ruby embarks upon a journey to rid herself of the damaging
emotional consequences of sexual abuse.

Sub Total $_____

Sales Tax 7.5% ($1.13 per book) $_____

Shipping/handling $_____
1st book, $2.50; each add'l. book $1.00 / U.S. orders only.
(For orders outside the United States, contact Wighita Press.)

TOTAL DUE $_____

PLEASE PRINT ALL INFORMATION.

Customer name: _____

Mailing address: _____

City/State/Zip: _____

Phone Number(s): _____

E-mail address: _____

**Make check or money order payable to Wighita Press and
mail order to:** P.O. Box 30399, Little Rock, Arkansas 72260-0399
Look for us on the web at: www.wighitapress.com   (501) 455-0905